SPY KIDS
ADVENTURES
OFF SIDES

D0061870

READ ALL THE SPY KIDS ADVENTURES!

OFF SIDES

Based on the characters
by Robert Rodriguez

Written by Elizabeth Lenhard

HYPERION
MIRAMAX BOOKS
New York

Printed in the United States of America

First Edition

1 3 5 7 9 10 8 6 4 2

This book is set in 13/17 New Baskerville.

ISBN 0-7868-0990-6

Visit www.spykids.com

CHAPTER 1

It was late at night and the Cortez household was utterly still. The cozy kitchen was dormant, the bedrooms were black, and nothing but shadows passed through the hallways.

Only in the cliff-top mansion's entertainment room was there even the slightest stirring—a flickering blue light. The light shuddered and shook, as if frightened by the horrible noises echoing through the room—moans and groans and howls, not to mention shrieks and screams and crunches!

Uh . . . crunches?

That would be the sound coming from Juni Cortez, snacking away on Cheezy Canoodles.

"I can't believe—*crunch, crunch*—that that guy is going into the garage," Juni said to his older sister, Carmen. He pointed a finger encrusted with orange cheese dust at the source of the flickering, blue light—a giant, flat-screen TV that was showing the movie *The Sand Witch Project*. This was movie

1

number twenty-three in Carmen and Juni's horror-movie marathon, which had been running for twelve nights straight.

On the TV, a pretty, young woman was leaving a raucous house party to get more soda from the garage.

"Doesn't she know—*crunch, munch*," Juni continued, "that when a character goes into a dark garage, a villain is surely lurking in the shadows, ready to attack?"

"Well, maybe she isn't as obsessed with horror movies as we are," Carmen said, reaching across the sofa to swipe some of Juni's Cheezy Canoodles.

Juni shoved a handful of potato chips into his mouth as the young woman on the screen opened the garage doors and tried to turn on the light.

"Of course. The bulb is burned out," Carmen said, without taking her eyes off the screen. "That's the first sign of impending doom. Now they're going to start the scary music."

Sure enough, an ominously low melody began to thrum from the TV speakers. Juni's eyes widened. In fact, he got so nervous he almost forgot to chew!

"Hmmm," the horror-movie girl said in a horrible, stagy voice. "Now, if I were a bottle of diet soda, where would I be? Hmmm . . . maybe in that closet over there."

"No!" Carmen cried gleefully. "Not the closet! It's the 'closet of doom,' right, Juni?"

Juni didn't answer.

His mouth is probably too full to talk, Carmen thought, rolling her eyes.

When Carmen refocused on the movie, the girl had, of course, entered the closet and was searching around in the dark for a flashlight. But before she could find it, a creepy man lunged out at her from behind a stack of shelves! He roared menacingly.

The girl screamed in horror.

The movie's sound track went shrill and screechy.

And the villain began chasing the girl around the garage.

"Run, minor character, run!" Carmen called out. Then she mumbled, "Not that it'll do you any good!"

Still staring at the scene, Carmen spoke out of the side of her mouth to her brother.

"I don't think this chase scene has quite the zip of that one in *Shriek VII*, do you?" she said. "And what was that flick we watched on day three of the horror-movie marathon? *The Arkansas Blender Brouhaha*? Now *that* was a chase scene, wasn't it, Juni? Uh . . . Juni?"

Her brother was completely silent. He wasn't even crunching any more. Finally, Carmen dragged her attention away from the television set and glanced at the other end of the couch. What she saw shocked her silly.

Juni had disappeared.

Carmen felt a bloodcurdling scream welling up inside her. She was just opening her mouth to let it out when suddenly, a logical thought hit her.

"Hello?" she muttered to herself. "You're simply under the influence of a scary movie. Juni probably just went to the kitchen to get more soda. Or he went to the bathroom. Or . . ."

Suddenly, Carmen noticed a large lump on the floor. The lump was covered by a pretty chenille afghan. It was trembling. And whimpering! And generally cowering in fear!

Carmen guffawed. Then she put the scary movie on PAUSE and jumped off the couch to rip the blanket off the lump—and found her brother curled up in a ball! Juni's round cheeks were ghostly pale, and his auburn curls were tangled and matted with sweat.

4

"I have two words for you, Juni Cortez," Carmen taunted. "Fraidy! Cat!"

"Don't call me names!" Juni yelled, jumping up. "Not unless you want me to remind you about day seven of the marathon. We weren't even five minutes into *Antlers!* when you started bawling."

"That was *so* different," Carmen protested, getting red in the face. "That was about a cute little animal that gets taken to outer space."

"Well, I have *two* words for you," Juni taunted. "Cry. Bab—"

"My point *is*," Carmen said, quickly changing the subject, "that it's crazy for *you* to be so scared by a movie. You're a Spy Kid. You know half a dozen different martial arts. You've jumped out of planes and free-climbed mountains. You've fought evil and won."

"Right back at ya, sis," Juni said sullenly.

Juni had a point. After all, Carmen was a spy, too! Together, the Cortez siblings worked for a top-secret government agency called the OSS—the Office of Strategic Services. Carmen and Juni saved the world as often as ordinary kids went to Little League practice. They took down villains with nothing more than their wits and a few high-tech gadgets. They could sense evil a mile away. And through the Spy Kids' work, villians were stopped before they could even start.

Of course, the Spy Kids hadn't always been spies. Once upon a time, they'd been two ordinary schoolkids, with two ordinary parents.

Or so they'd thought!

In fact, the Spy Kids' mom and dad—Ingrid and Gregorio Cortez—had been retired spies! And the bedtime stories they told Carmen and Juni about death-defying missions were actually true!

Once upon a time (according to the kids' favorite story), Ingrid and Gregorio were the most dangerous spies in the world. They were mortal enemies. Ingrid's spy agency had even ordered her to take Gregorio out. And on the very same day, Gregorio was told to eliminate Ingrid.

But the mission changed when the ruthless spies finally met. Instead of assassinating each other, they fell in love! They then embarked upon one of the most dangerous adventures of all— marriage.

When Carmen and Juni were born, a few years later, things started getting complicated for Ingrid and Gregorio. They didn't like leaving their kids with babysitters while they went off to save the world. And it didn't seem responsible to be dodging bullets and kicking butt when there was laundry to do and diapers to change at home.

So, the elder Cortezes dropped out of the spy biz. They began working at home, as ordinary consultants. And Carmen and Juni were none the wiser.

Until one day, years later, when the OSS called upon Ingrid and Gregorio again. Several of the agency's best spies had been abducted by an evil children's entertainer named Fegan Floop. The Cortez parents were asked to save them.

The only problem was that all those years behind a desk had made the grown-up spies a little sloppy. They were only minutes into their mission when they were captured.

Carmen and Juni had found out their parents were imprisoned and leaped into action. They saved their parents, saved the world, and changed their own lives forever. They became spies, too.

Now, all four Cortezes worked for the OSS. Together they were an extraordinary team.

But that didn't mean they didn't have a few ordinary weaknesses.

"Yes," Carmen was saying now, as she flicked on the light in the shadowy entertainment room, "it *is* ridiculous for an international superspy to be scared of a movie. But then again, why should I be surprised? You used to get so scared that your sweaty hands were covered in warts! Ewwww!"

"You know I haven't had sweaty palms or warts in forever!" Juni growled. "Can't you just let it go?"

"Sure," Carmen giggled. "Maybe I'll forget by the time you, say, graduate from college!"

"No fair, Carmen!" Juni howled. "If you don't stop dissing me, right now, I'll . . . I'll . . ."

Ah-WHOOP! Ah-WHOOP! Ah-WHOOP!

A blaring siren had just cut Juni off. And a red light over the entertainment-room door had begun flashing wildly. It was the OSS call to action!

"Whoops!" Carmen said with a grin. "Guess I'm free to dis you for a while longer. Or at least until after our next mission! Let's go see what it is!"

CHAPTER 2

Carmen and Juni ran out of the room and dashed up the stairs. The sound of the alarm finally subsided when the kids reached the long, dark, upstairs hallway.

"Mom? Dad?" Carmen called down the hall.

"We're in our bedroom, Carmenita," Dad called out in his deep, Spanish-accented voice. Carmen and Juni rushed down the corridor and burst through their parents' bedroom door. Then they recoiled in horror!

Mom and Dad were sitting on their bed, propped up against a mountain of frilly pillows. They were watching a movie of their own on the bedroom TV. But it wasn't an action-packed spy thriller or a horror movie. No, it was a romantic comedy, complete with soft music, flattering lighting, and kissing!

But that wasn't all. Mom and Dad were also

snacking on saltless, oil-free popcorn! *And* they were holding hands!

"Mushy stuff!" Carmen cried in despair.

"And healthy snack food!" Juni added with a sneer. "Please, Mom and Dad. There are children present. Could you have some consideration?"

"Sorry, kids," Mom said in her sweet, raspy voice. With a sigh of regret, she dropped her husband's hand and aimed the remote at the television to turn it off. "And we were just getting to the good part—where the hero runs through the streets of New York to catch his lady love before she boards a train. I'm sure there would have been a big kiss at the end."

"Ewww!" both Spy Kids blurted out in unison.

"Don't be so hard on your mother," Dad said, winking at his children as he got out of bed and stood. "Romantic comedies are her weakness."

"Oh, really, Gregorio?" Mom said. She jumped off the bed to stand next to her husband, hands on her hips. "A girl thing, huh?"

"*Sí,*" Dad said, chucking Mom's chin playfully. "Don't worry, honey. I think it's cute."

"Oh, I'll give you *cute,*" Mom said. She grabbed Dad's arm and pulled it over her shoulder at a precise angle. Before Dad knew it, Mom had flipped him into the air! He sailed about five feet up before landing on the bed with a startled grunt.

"Ingrid!" he gasped. "What was that?"

"Oh, a new martial-arts move I learned at OSS training last week," Mom said. "It works best when the fighter is several inches shorter than her foe. It's the perfect male-to-female combat tool."

"Let me guess, Mom," Carmen said with a giggle. "This martial-arts move? Is it called—"

"A Girl Thing," Mom finished, her green eyes flashing mischievously. "However did you guess, Carmen?"

"All right, all right," Dad grumbled as he slumped off the bed. "If you ladies are done laughing, I believe we have a call from the OSS to answer."

Mom and Carmen stifled their giggles while Dad grabbed the remote control. He aimed it at the television and hit the POWER button. When the screen flickered to life, Mom and Dad's romantic movie was gone. In its place was the spies' boss—Diego Devlin.

Usually, Devlin addressed the Cortezes from behind his big, executive desk. He'd be looking dapper in a crisp suit and slicked-back hair. He was the head of the OSS—a post that was all about dignity.

But, today, he was wearing baggy, royal-blue shorts, kneesocks, shin guards, and cleats! He was bouncing a soccer ball from hand to hand as his spies tuned in. When he saw that he had the Cortezes' attention, he tossed the ball into the air, then bopped it across his office with his head.

Or, to be more specific, his nose! Devlin yelped as the ball whomped him in the face. He quickly clapped his hand over his bruised beak.

"Oooh!" Juni said with a cringe. "That's gotta hurt, Mr. Devlin."

"Sure does!" Devlin said nasally. "I suddenly have a whole new respect for soccer players."

"See?" Dad said proudly. "Haven't I been telling you this very thing for years, Devlin? European football—what you Americans like to call soccer—is the coolest sport on earth. Much better than that *other* football game, you know, the one with the weird, pointy pigskin and all that padding under the players' uniforms."

"Well, you may have finally made your point with me, Gregorio," Devlin said, prodding his nose painfully. Then he turned to the younger spies. "Let me ask you this, kids. Do you feel the same way about socc—uh, football?"

"Totally!" Juni said, lifting his fist in the air. "I've been playing soccer since I was six."

"Me, too," Carmen said. "Soccer's up there with skydiving and computer hacking on my list of fave activities."

"Good," Devlin said. "Because your next mission is going to require a major love of the game. And an airline ticket to Scotland!"

"Scotland?" Juni gasped. "As in the site of the next International Soccer Competition? You mean, *that* Scotland?"

Devlin scooped his soccer ball off the office floor and grinned out of the television at the now very excited young spy.

"You got it," he said enthusiastically. "The International Soccer Competition happens only once every four years. It's enough to make even Americans excited about the sport."

To emphasize his point, Devlin began juggling his ball in the air with his knees. Of course, Devlin bopped the ball only a few times before it flew out of his control again. It shot out of the Cortezes' view—but not out of their range of hearing!

Crasssshhh! Tinkle-tinkle-tinkle.

"Oooh," Carmen said with a cringe. "Sounds like that was a lamp, Mr. Devlin."

"And a picture frame," Devlin admitted with a sigh. "But my office is not your concern. You've got bigger wrecks to deal with."

"And that wreck would be?" Carmen asked respectfully.

"Only the future of soccer in America altogether," Devlin said gravely.

"I don't understand!" Juni exclaimed. "The American All-Stars are doing great. They even made it to the finals of the International Soccer Competition next week. They're facing off against the Scottish team, Brogue United. What's gone wrong, Mr. Devlin?"

"That's what we need to find out," Devlin said. "You see, something's extremely wacky in the new Scottish soccer stadium."

"Oooh, I read about that place," Carmen said. "The United Kingdom invested millions in this fancy new stadium up in the Scottish Highlands. It took four whole years to build the thing. It's supposed to be monstrous!"

"Interesting choice of words, Carmen," Devlin replied drily. "That's exactly how the All-Stars are finding it. Every time they hit the field to practice, they're terrorized by unseen forces—scares of the most supernatural kind. Our team's players have been bewitched and bothered. Now, they're more than bewildered—they're completely freaked."

"A rebellious stadium," Juni said, putting a finger to his chin. "Mr. Devlin? Let me guess—do the players try to sit down on the bench, only to have it yanked out from beneath them? Or do they see their soccer balls deflate before their eyes, and trip on wires that weren't there a moment ago? Stuff like that?"

"Juni!" Devlin said, raising his thick eyebrows. "I'm impressed. You must be taking that mind-reading class at the OSS Spy Kid school."

"Nah," Juni said modestly. "It was just a hunch, really. You see, this situation sounds just like one of my favorite horror movies, *Houseghost!* It's all about some unwanted 'visitors' who take over a house and, at one point, a football field."

Devlin's eyebrows rose sky-high.

Mom covered a smile with her hand while Dad harrumphed quietly.

Carmen rolled her eyes and sighed in disgust.

I can't believe it, she thought in exasperation. Juni actually just suggested that the stadium was haunted! That's only, like, the *least* scientific and *most* babyish explanation he could have come up with. How totally unspylike!

Devlin's reaction was a bit more diplomatic.

"Well, Juni," he said with a small smile. "A ghost. That's an . . . interesting theory. But, you see, son, in my many years of dealing with evildoers, searching for secrets, and doing away with double agents, I've learned one thing. Behind every mystery is a mysterymonger—a *human being*—with a plan and, usually, the high-tech gadgets to make it happen. Ghosts, haunted houses, the Loch Ness monster— that's all a bunch of hooey."

"Hollywood hooey," Dad added.

"I couldn't agree more," a red-faced Carmen said. "So, Mr. Devlin, what's our intel on this mystery *person?*"

Carmen gave her brother a pointed look as she posed the question.

"Well, actually, Carmen," Devlin said sheepishly, "we've got next to nothing on this person. His or her mischief is so high-tech our OSS satellites can't find a single source for it. That's why it's time to send in our best spies. We need you and Juni to go to the stadium and get to the bottom of this mystery. Your parents will stay home to receive your intel and run it through analysis."

"We'll leave in the morning, sir," Carmen said, with the utmost professionalism.

"We're going to Scotland!" Juni yelled, with slightly less professionalism. "We're taking a transatlantic airplane ride. And then we get to hang out with famous soccer players. This is gonna be *so* cool!"

Mom stepped toward the television, gazing at her boss with a look of concern.

"I'm sorry, Devlin," she said to the boss, who was now attempting to dribble his soccer ball across the office floor. "With all due respect, we're talking about a *game* here. Sabotaging a soccer game is definitely not very sporting. But is it really a situation that requires international superspies? I mean, we usually save the world. It sounds like you're talking about playing referee."

"Excellent point, Ingrid," Devlin said. "I'll explain. You see, the American Soccer League is the most mocked team in the entire world of football."

As Devlin said this, his soccer ball careened out of control again, knocking over a potted plant this time.

He looked at the family sheepishly. "As I was saying, if the Americans forfeit in the International Soccer Competition, there'll be widespread outrage. Everyone loves soccer."

"That would be a horrible forfeiture!" Dad said, growing white.

"Yeah," Juni agreed. "A total bummer."

"Oh, I think it'd be much more than a bummer," Devlin said grimly. "It'd be this mystery villain's first step."

"Toward what?" Carmen wondered.

"I think this criminal wants to chip away at American activities, bit by bit," Devlin said. "He'll start with an easy target—soccer. But who knows? From there, he might go on to sabotage the baseball or movie business."

"No more romantic comedies?" Mom gasped.

"Or he could target the fast-food industry," Devlin suggested.

"No more Big Whop Burgers?" Juni cried in alarm.

"Or even malls," Devlin said ominously.

"Malls?" Carmen shrieked.

"Well, now that I've gotten your attention," Devlin said, scooping up his soccer ball and placing it firmly upon his desk, "I think you'd better start packing. It's a long trip to Scotland, and you kids are on the next flight out!"

CHAPTER 3

The next afternoon found Carmen and Juni staggering out of the airport in Scotland's capital, Edinburgh. Carmen felt every bit the tattered traveler. Her OSS uniform—cool, black cargo pants and a pocket-laden utility vest, plus a lime-green, long-sleeved T-shirt—was horribly wrinkled. She was bleary-eyed and jet-lagged because of the eight-hour time difference.

Juni, on the other hand, was aggrieved only by the past eight hours of airline food.

"Ugh," he said, clutching his stomach. "I feel like I ate a couple of bricks!"

"You might as well have," Carmen said accusingly. "At lunch alone you downed three pies, fried potato balls, and a fruitcake."

"Hey, I was just trying to be a good spy," Juni protested.

"Oh, really?" Carmen said, rolling her eyes.

"Since when does snacking yourself into a stupor count as spying?"

"I was learning about the cuisine of this foreign land," Juni said, gesturing toward the road abutting the airport. Squashy British cars were zipping by driving on the left side of the road. "Know thine enemy, right?"

"Aye, so that's what you think of us Scots, is it?" said someone in a chipper voice behind the Spy Kids. They jumped and whirled around to face a young man with rosy cheeks, blond curls, and laughing blue eyes.

"Carmen and Juni Corrrrrr-tez, I prrrrr-esume," the guy said, rolling his Rs in a thick Scottish brogue.

"How did you know?" Juni said.

"I got a call from yer parents," the young man said. "They told me to look for two shorrrrrt spies. Said ye'd probably be bickering when I saw you. Boy, did they have that rrrright."

Carmen and Juni's faces turned bright red. One of the first rules of spying was: Never allow yourself to be easily spotted in a crowd. The Spy Kids shot each other a chagrined glance, then looked morosely at their shoes.

"Aw, cheer up," the strange man said, simultaneously patting each kid's shoulder. "I never would have spotted ye, if I weren't a spy meself, I swear it to ye."

"Oh!" Carmen said, looking up at the man shyly. "Well, that makes me feel a little bit better. So you're with the OSS's U.K. branch?"

"I am, I am," the man said. He extended both arms to the kids for a two-fisted handshake. "Macauley M. MacDonald, at yer service."

MacDonald grabbed the kids' bags and strode down the sidewalk toward a battered old car parked by the curb. Carmen and Juni hurried after him.

"Yer mum and pop asked me to drive you to the soccer stadium," Macdonald continued. "It's a three-hour trip through ourrrrr craggy highlands. Ye'd surrrrely get lost if ye tried it on yer own."

"Oh, really?" Carmen said, stopping in her tracks to plant her fists determinedly on her hips. "I'll have you know I'm famous at the OSS for my supreme navigational skills."

"Yeh, yer mum said you'd say that," MacDonald said, grinning and tossing the kids' bags into his trunk. "Said ye were a stubborn one. And that you, Juni, would be wantin' something ter eat. Well, don't worry, we'll be stoppin' fer some dinner in about an hour. I'm gonna treat ye bairns to a Scottish delicacy—haggis!"

"*What?*" Juni asked, his voice trembling.

"*Great chieftain o' the pudden race,*" MacDonald said. "At least, that's what me favorite poet, Robbie Burns, said about haggis. And why not, I ask ye? What's not to love about sheep's heart, liver, and lungs, tucked into the sheep's stomach with a bit o' oatmeal, and boiled for a few hours. Ye never tasted anything like it, I assure ye."

"Ewww," Juni groaned, clutching his stomach.

"No kidding," Carmen whispered to her brother as MacDonald zipped into traffic and headed out of the city. "That to me sounds pretty scary."

A few hours into the car trip, MacDonald was filling the Spy Kids in. In fact, he was just now finishing a Scottish ghost story. He told it in a dark and creepy voice as he swerved down a dark and creepy country road.

"And so," he was saying, "the brother and sister plunged into the loch. They couldn't help themselves, ye see? They had heard such grand tales about the city of ghosts on the loch's floor, they just *had* to see it for themselves.

"Perhaps they made it to that legendary city,"

MacDonald continued. "Perhaps they didn't. We'll never know. Because they were never heard from again!"

As the story ended, MacDonald's voice returned to its normal, chipper brogue.

"And that's the tale of the city of ghosts and the lost O'Shanaghan siblings," he said. "Good one, isn't it? Me mum used to tell us that one before we went to bed."

"Your *mother* told you that?" Juni quavered. "Our mom would never tell us such a scary story. Especially not before bed. That's just *asking* for nightmares!"

"Well, yeah!" MacDonald said innocently. "That's part o' the fun, isn't it? Ye see, we Scots love our ghost stories. Can't get enough of 'em. Luckily, we've got no shortage of scary sources. Creepy lochs. Mysterious piles of ancient stones. And hundreds of crumbling, old castles—haunted, every one."

"Really?" Juni squeaked.

"Sure!" MacDonald said cheerfully, seemingly unaware of the effect his news was having on Juni.

"MacDonald," Carmen said, trying to sound brisk and rational, despite the slight wobble in her voice. "You *are* joking about all this, aren't you? I mean, it's OSS policy that ghosts and haunted castles and the Loch Ness monster are just stories."

"Yeah, I know the policy," MacDonald said. "But I also know the truth. Maybe you will, too, by the end of this mission."

With that, MacDonald fell silent, except for the mournful, Scottish song that he began to whistle as he drove deeper and deeper into the dark and rocky countryside.

Juni looked at his sister with a terrified glance.

"You don't seriously think," he whispered, "that MacDonald really means his ghost stories are true, do you?"

For a moment, Carmen wasn't so sure. But then, she shook her head stubbornly. She was a spy, not a fool.

"Well, of course they're not true," she said. "MacDonald's just trying to entertain us. Pretend that this is just another horror movie we are watching on TV."

"Yeah, a 3-D one!" Juni whimpered, glancing out the window into the inky night.

"Listen," Carmen whispered. "MacDonald said only one thing you should pay attention to: we'll know the truth by the end of our *mission*. That's what we're here for. But I don't need to do any spying to know that there's a perfectly reasonable explanation behind the 'city of ghosts' and creepy castles *and* the 'haunted stadium.' You'll see it, too—after you've had a good night's sleep."

No sooner had the words left Carmen's mouth than MacDonald's compact car screeched to a halt.

"Well, here we are at your hotel," MacDonald announced. He jumped out of the car and hauled the kids' bags out of the trunk. "You must be tired. I'll be on my way, so you can check in and get some rest. You can walk to the stadium in the morning. It's just down the lane a wee bit."

"Sweet! Thanks for the ride—and the stories— MacDonald," Carmen said. She stepped out of the car with Juni close behind her. They started to let out a collective sigh of relief—until they looked up at their hotel!

The building was made of ancient, wind-worn, gray stone. It had tiny windows, glowing with ominous, flickering candlelight. The hotel had a turret on every corner and ramparts on the roof. It even had a drawbridge.

The Spy Kids would be staying in a drafty, old castle, after all, just like the ones in MacDonald's terrifying ghost stories.

"Now, this is a real Scottish landmark,"

MacDonald said, gazing up at the hotel affectionately. "This castle is at least four hundred years old. It's a drafty old wreck. But don't worry—there's a fireplace in every room, and hot water in every faucet. There's *also* a story behind the place. It involves a jilted bride, a full moon, and a butcher knife. Ahem—Once upon a ti—"

"You know, MacDonald," Carmen interrupted desperately, "as much as I'd love to hear another ghost story, I don't think we have time. Y'see, Juni's got to get to bed. Just look at him—he's wiped out!"

Carmen pointed at Juni. His eyes were open so wide they were bulging. His fists were clenched. His teeth were chattering, and his knees were knocking.

"Huh, he looks wide-awake ter me!" MacDonald said, gazing quizzically at the petrified Spy Boy.

"Oh, no, trust me," Carmen said, grabbing Juni's shoulder and leading him toward the hotel and away from another potential ghost story. "He'll be snoring away, soon. So, uh, thanks for the ride, MacDonald! See you around."

"No problem, Carmen," MacDonald said, happily waving good-bye to the kids. "You get that ghostie in the stadium, y'hear!"

"You bet," Carmen squeaked, laughing weakly. Meanwhile, Juni's eyes got even bulgier.

As MacDonald's car roared away, the kids stepped through a heavy door into the hotel lobby—a stony, dungeonlike foyer lined with dusty tapestries, suits of ancient armor, cobwebs, and shadows. It was dank, and it was cold.

"A good night's sleep, huh?" Juni said, gaping at the dreary digs and shivering. "Let's hope all the ghosts are asleep, too."

CHAPTER 4

The next morning, the sleepy Spy Kids stumbled into the hotel's drafty dining room for a quick breakfast of thick, stick-to-your-ribs porridge. Then they hiked down a rocky lane to the stadium. When they arrived they sighed forlornly.

"Looks like another castle," Carmen said, gazing up at the giant arena.

"Another *haunted* castle," Juni mumbled.

Carmen couldn't contradict him. The bowl-shaped stadium had been built of old, weather-beaten stone bricks. The press box was situated in an old widow's walk. Round turrets housed the VIP seats. The place was just as creepy as the kids' old hotel.

"Aye, admiring Brogue United's new digs, are ye?" said a voice behind the kids. They turned to face a man in little spectacles, a woolly, gray cap, and a tweed blazer. He was holding a walking stick. He'd clearly been hiking through the grassy hills when he'd happened upon the Spy Kids. "Yep, building this stadium was quite a feat. Want to know how they did it?" the man asked eagerly.

"Uh, I guess so," Juni said, with a note of apprehension in his voice.

There better not be any ghosts in *this* story, he thought.

"Tore down about a dozen ancient, Scottish castles, they did," the man said proudly.

"What?" Carmen gasped. "Aren't those castles historic landmarks or something? Shouldn't they be protected?"

"Achh, the country's full of castles," the man said with a shrug. "A few less won't do anybody any harm. The things were coming apart at the seams, anyway. Would've collapsed completely in another century or so."

"Well, in that case . . ." Carmen said sarcastically.

"Americans," the man scoffed jovially. "Your country's so young you think every old thing is a treasure. But, think about it. Buildings are meant for people. And those old castles weren't fit to house anybody—except for ghosties, perhaps."

At this, a mischievous smile flitted across the stranger's face. And a look of panic settled on Juni's.

"Come to think of it," the man said, "there were probably lots of spirits who made their homes in those old wrecks. And they were probably none too pleased when their homes were stolen away from them, eh? Maybe they're haunting the Stand-Off Stadium right now. . . . Boo!"

Juni jumped and let out an involuntary squeak. The man laughed good-naturedly.

"I knew that'd entertain you," he said. "All children like a good scare, eh?"

"I'm beginning to think that theory is not quite true," Juni grumbled. Carmen merely nodded, said good-bye, and shook the man's hand. He turned and continued on his hike.

Now, it was mission time. The kids took a couple of deep breaths as they stalked up to the stadium and passed through the drawbridge. When they emerged, they gasped. They were gazing around the largest, most amazing arena they'd ever seen! The stadium's façade might have been creaky and castlelike, but inside, it was thoroughly modern. The empty bleachers were terraced; the snack stands were swank, and the playing field was a dazzling, emerald green. And at that particular moment, the field was bustling with soccer players in stylish, brightly colored uniforms.

"Those are Brogue United players out on the pitch," Juni noted, pointing at the footballers' red jerseys as he settled himself into a front-row seat. "They must be practicing a scrimmage."

"The pitch?" Carmen said, sitting next to Juni.

"Yeah, that's the British term for 'playing field,'" Juni said. "MacDonald told me that yesterday."

"Did he also tell you about a certain *pitch-dark* night haunted by a *ghoulish ghost?*" Carmen asked, waggling her fingers at Juni and lowering her voice until it took on a sinister note.

"No!" Juni cried, going white. "And I don't want to hear about it!"

"I was kidding!" Carmen said. "Seriously, Juni. You are way too spooked by this scary Scotland thing. It's just a legend the locals use to tease themselves and the tourists. Like alligators in the sewers of New York or Sasquatch in Alaska."

"Yeah," Juni grumbled, folding his arms over his stomach. "Well, I'm not so sure those aren't real, too."

Carmen took a seat next to Juni. "Okay, enough supernatural talk. It's time to start spying."

The Spy Kids' eyes followed the Brogue United players as they dashed around the field. The athletes were stocky and squat, with legs as thick as logs. They were communicating to each other in guttural tones.

"Hey!" a fullback screamed at one of the mid-fielders. "Watch yer back!"

The midfielder responded by passing the ball to a forward, screaming, "Shoot it, ye big lout!"

The forward scowled at the midfielder. But he did as he was told and kicked. He *scored*!

"Whoa!" Carmen said. "Those guys are tough."

"Well, the members of Brogue United are notoriously surly," Juni said with a shrug. "Some people say they simply bullied their way into the International Soccer Competition finals."

"I can believe it," Carmen said. "These guys are a bunch of beasts. . . ."

Carmen's voice trailed off as she spotted a player leaving the bench and bounding onto the field to join the scrimmage. He looked nothing like his teammates. While they were brusque and burly, he was lean and lithe. They had closely cropped, scrubby hair. His was long, blond, and silky. His chin was chiseled, his nose was noble, and his eyes were a sparkling blue. He loped around the field, dribbling the ball with an effortless grace.

He was the most glamorous athlete Carmen had ever seen. Not to mention the hottest.

"*Who* is that?" she breathed.

Juni rolled his eyes.

Here we go, he thought. Carmen gets another crush.

Irritably, Juni explained the situation to his sister. "That's Dirk Beckon! He's one of the world's most fabulous footballers. He's a spokesmodel for Spikē Sportswear and Big Whop Burgers. And he *used* to be the most eligible bachelor in Europe, but then he married Cozy Clove."

"The movie actress?" Carmen gasped. "Wow! She was in at least three films in our horror-movie marathon! She's megafamous."

"She's also right there!" Juni said suddenly. He pointed excitedly to one of the VIP turrets. Cozy Clove Beckon—wearing a tight, white pantsuit and large, blue-tinted sunglasses—was just striding into the suite of seats. Trailing her was an entourage of publicists, agents, stylists, and fans. But despite all the attention—not to mention all the activity on the soccer field—Cozy looked sullen and bored. In fact, as the members of Brogue United continued their practice, the Spy Kids saw her sigh and yawn obnoxiously.

Finally, the practice ended and the players left the field. Cozy immediately jumped out of her seat and flounced off to meet her husband, her hangers-on in tow.

While Carmen stared in awe at the departing star, Juni looked at his spy watch. In addition to being a complex computer, navigational system, satellite communications hub, *and* treasure trove of minivideo games, the handy-dandy device also told time.

"Okay," he said. "It's just about time for the American All-Stars to start their practice. Let's see if anything weird happens."

The Spy Kids held their breath as the blue-shirted Americans began to trot onto the field. At first, they passed and dribbled the ball tentatively. They were clearly spooked by their recent scares.

But when the team had played for a full fifteen minutes, mishap-free, their confidence grew. They began shooting more aggressively and jumping into the air to hit showy headers. In fact, they began playing brilliantly!

"They're on fire!" Juni cried.

"Tscha!" Carmen agreed. After the kids had watched the practice for a couple more minutes, Carmen wrinkled her nose.

"Do you smell that?" she asked her brother. "It's almost like—"

"—The All-Stars are *literally* on fire!" Juni cried, jumping to his feet. He pointed to a corner of the playing field. A dancing, foot-tall flame had suddenly erupted on one of the sidelines. Now it was chasing down a midfielder. The frightened footballer began shrieking and darting back and forth across the pitch. He veered to the left, leaped to the right, and even did a sloppy somersault. But the flame would not be deflected.

"It's a ghost!" Juni cried.

"It's *not* a ghost!" Carmen retorted, jumping to her feet. "It's some super-high-tech haunting perpetrated by a big, bad villain. And *we're* gonna get to the bottom of it. Come on!"

The Spy Kids vaulted over the bleachers' guardrail, landing on the pitch with catlike grace. They began to chase after the darting flame. As they pounded across the field, Juni yelled at his sister, "So, any thoughts on how we are gonna beat this blaze?"

"Oh," Carmen said, smiling slyly as she ran, "I think we need some help from our favorite uncle!"

"Uncle Machete?" Juni said skeptically. "Uh, no offense, Carmen, but that's the worst idea I ever heard. By the time Uncle Machete makes it all the way from his gadget workshop to Scotland, the stadium will be a big, smoking, pile of nothing!"

Carmen glared at her brother. "The 'help' I was referring to is a stash of Uncle Machete–made gizmos!"

"Oh," Juni said. As he jogged beside her, he watched Carmen pull a trove of crime-fighting gizmos out of her vest pocket. The sight gave Juni a small measure of comfort.

Why only a small measure?

Well, Uncle Machete was a brilliant inventor. For every spy maneuver, he had a gadget—from rocket shoes to sucker soles to supernatural disguises. Though Uncle Machete's ideas were always fabulous, his finished products were sometimes not so fabulous. On their many missions, Carmen and Juni had suffered through a lot of glitchy gadgets, like the horrible-tasting Huffenpuff Hot-Air Pills, and the Reversible Hair Dye, which ended up only reversing hair to pink-and-green stripes!

But even with their embarrassing faults, Uncle Machete's gadgets were often lifesavers. So Juni had his small comfort.

"What do ya got?" he called to Carmen.

"How about we zap the flame with some Insta-Ice?" Carmen called, holding up an iridescent, blue device that looked like a squirt gun.

Juni shook his head.

"Remember when we tried to use that thing to cool off on our mission in the Sahara Desert?" he said. "The zapper's aim was totally off."

"Oh, yeah," Carmen recalled, cringing. "Boy, was that camel mad! Okay, how about—"

Carmen paused to hold up a small, green tube.

"—Some Super Sweat?"

"That's a new one," Juni said. "What's it do?"

"You'll see!" Carmen declared. She flipped a cap off the little tube to reveal a spray button. Then she aimed the button at Juni and began spritzing him with warm liquid.

"Hey!" Juni complained as the slimy stuff settled onto his skin. "How come *I'm* always the guinea pig?"

"Because you're so good at it!" Carmen replied.

"Oh!" Juni said in surprise. "Thanks. I'm glad you've finally come to appreciate my spy skills. Hey, wait a minute. What's happening to me?"

Juni looked down at his hands. They were dripping with sweat. His legs were clammy with per-spiration, too! And his face was squirting so much salty stuff that he could barely see. Juni skidded to a halt on the soccer field.

"Carmen!" he roared. "I just figured out what Super Sweat is! You . . . you . . ."

"Hey, Drippy," Carmen yelled. "Stop wasting

time and go sweat on that sizzler!"

Juni scowled at his sister. He had to admit that her idea was an excellent one. He resumed running after the dancing flame, which was still chasing after the hapless soccer player. In his anger, Juni ran so fast that he quickly caught up with the fire. He flicked his dripping hands at the flame, shook his soaked hair over it, and kicked at it with his damp legs.

All of the stinky sweat pouring off Juni's body overpowered the fire. Finally, the flame went out, with a wet-sounding fizzle.

"Whoo-hoo!" called out several of the All-Stars, who'd been cowering on the sidelines during the fire fiasco.

Juni waved at them proudly, spewing gobs of sweat as he did. The players' faces turned instantly from relieved to repelled.

"Okay," Juni muttered to himself, a bit offended. "So I have a little perspiration problem. You'd think professional athletes wouldn't be so queasy about it!"

Only when the players screamed and pointed over Juni's shoulder did the Spy Kid realize that maybe he wasn't what the players were freaked out by. Juni spun around. Sure enough, another haunt had struck! The goalie had just been scooped up in the soccer net! Now the net was bucking and flailing, tossing the poor man around like a snared fish! Carmen was already on the case, running to the man's rescue.

Juni was just starting to run after Carmen when, suddenly, one of the chalk lines on the pitch reared up into the air. Somehow, the once-flaky line had gone solid. And it tripped Juni in midsprint!

At the sight of Juni sprawled on the ground, one of the All-Stars on the sidelines screamed, "That's it! I'm outta here!"

"Don't leave without me!" cried one of his teammates.

Even the coaches were ready to bail. Pretty soon, every last American—save the hapless goalie and the two spies—had fled the stadium.

Feeling more than a little bruised, Juni picked himself up off the pitch and whipped a collapsible pogo stick out of his vest pocket. Unfolding the pogo stick to full size with a loud *sproing*, Juni began to hop across the field, deftly dodging the moving chalk lines.

By the time he reached Carmen, she'd pulled out her acid crayon and begun to burn away the goal net. A few seconds later, the goalie was free.

"Thanks!" he said to Carmen breathlessly. "You're a brave girl!"

"I'm a spy," Carmen corrected him. "Just doing my job."

"Well," the goalie replied, glancing around nervously, "you won't be needing me then, will you? See ya!"

The player began running toward the stadium exit, screaming to his retreating teammates, "Wait for meeeeeee!"

That left Carmen and Juni alone in the mammoth arena. When Juni spoke, his voice echoed eerily.

"What should we do now?" he asked his sister.

"Look for clues, of course," Carmen replied.

"I thought that's what you'd say," Juni said, with a sigh of resignation. "I'll go check out the chalk lines. You see if you can find the source of that flame."

"Roger," Carmen said. The Spy Kids were just beginning to walk to opposite ends of the field when suddenly, Juni's cell phone rang with a shrill *beeeeep*!

"That must be Mom and Dad," he said with a grin. "They're the only ones who have my cell phone number. Wait'll they hear about what's been going on over on this side of the Atlantic."

Juni quickly dug the cell phone out of his pocket and looked at its caller ID screen, expecting to see his home digits. Instead, he saw a number he didn't recognize.

"Hey, who's this?" Juni asked as he hit the phone's TALK button. He held the phone to his ear. "Hello?"

"Juni Cortez," said a strange, hissing voice on the phone. The sound sent shivers down Juni's spine.

"Yes?" Juni squeaked.

"You'll never find me!" the voice rasped. "Even though I'm right within your reach."

"What are you talking about?" Juni cried. With a puzzled look, Carmen trotted over to Juni's side and cocked her head toward his to listen in.

"Where are you calling from?" Juni squeaked into the phone.

"From *inside the stadium*!" the creepy voice crowed. The line went dead.

Juni gasped and spun around, scanning the bleachers with wide eyes. They were empty! There wasn't a soul to be seen.

Juni pressed END on his cell phone with trembling fingers.

"Carmen?" he quavered. "Remember movie number thirteen in our marathon?"

"*The Babysitter,*" Carmen squeaked back, "where the bad guy calls the babysitter from inside the house?"

"Yeah!" Juni cried. He took a shaky breath. "Well, this scenario is starting to feel just like that!"

Carmen tried to access her scientific sense of logic. Her mathematical precision. Her deep-down belief that ghosts did not exist.

But she totally failed! Instead, she did something very un-Carmen-like. Looking seriously at Juni, she scowled and then screamed, "Run!"

CHAPTER 5

The Spy Kids sprinted out of the stadium.

They ran down the gravelly country lane that led back to town.

They jogged up the town's quaint main street.

And finally, they slumped onto a bench on the sidewalk. They were shocked, angry, weary, and (in Juni's case, anyway) very, very sweaty.

"I *dare* you to tell me," Juni said as he flicked a hank of wet curls off his forehead, "that that stadium isn't haunted by a real ghost."

"Fine, I'll tell you," Carmen retorted weakly. "That was not a real ghost. That was the work of a villain."

"A really *scary* guy," Juni added.

"I'll give you that," Carmen said. "Which means, we have good news!"

"Yeah, right!"

"We do," Carmen insisted. "The good news is that now we know what we're up against. The next time we face off with this villain, we'll know what to expect. So . . . we won't be scared. It's as simple as that."

"Uh-huh," Juni said, hauling himself to his feet. "That's an excellent *theory*, Carmen. Let's see if it'll actually hold water the next time I'm chased down by a runaway fire!"

"Huh," Carmen sniffed. "Maybe I'm just made of stronger stuff than you. *Spy* stuff, to be exact."

"Hey!" Juni cried. "Take that back!"

"Or what?" Carmen taunted.

"Or I'll make you eat those words," Juni said.

"Well, you *are* the expert on eating," Carmen replied.

"Well *you're* a know-it-all, and, and . . ."

Suddenly, Juni (who *was* an expert on eating) was distracted by a delicious, meaty scent that came wafting beneath his nose. He looked around the pub with hungry eyes. Directly over his head, he discovered a weather-beaten sign that read: MACKINTOSH'S PUB, HOME OF THE BEST COLCANNON AND CROWDIES THE HIGHLANDS HAVE TO OFFER!

"Colcannon," Juni breathed, his argument with Carmen forgotten. "And crowdies. Yum!"

"Do you even know what that is?" Carmen scoffed.

"No, but it's *gotta* be better than haggis," Juni said, licking his lips. "Let's get some lunch. We can strategize while we eat."

"Like I said," Carmen said, rolling her eyes, "you're the expert."

She followed Juni into the pub without a word. After the morning's strenuous spying, *her* stomach was grumbling, too.

The spies were seated at a cozy, wooden table set with a darkly flickering oil lamp and napkins as big as hand towels. A few minutes later they were served a steaming meal of colcannon.

Juni eyed his colcannon suspiciously before taking a tentative bite. As he swallowed, though, he grinned in delight.

"Finally," he announced, "a mystery that isn't totally terrifying. Colcannon is just a stew of cabbage, carrots, and buttered potatoes. It's totally yummy!"

"This smoked salmon is pretty good, too!" Carmen said, taking a big bite of the fish on a piece of fragrant black bread.

Soon, Carmen and Juni began to feel warmer, fuller, and slightly less freaked. They began to mull over the next step in their spying.

"Y'see, Juni," Carmen said, dabbing at the

corners of her mouth with her napkin, "you've got to start by looking at the facts. Nobody, over the entire course of humanity, has ever been able to prove that ghosts exist. And thus, they don't! The only believers are people like you, who let their imaginations run away with them."

Juni scowled. But before he could issue a snide comeback, both spies were distracted by a commotion at the pub door. A throng of men with cameras was backing into the restaurant. Flashbulbs popped like fireflies as the photographers jostled one another, fighting to get the perfect picture.

Carmen and Juni hopped onto their chairs to peer into the cluster of paparazzi.

"It's Cozy Beckon!" Carmen gasped.

The star was smiling dazzlingly for the cameras. But after a few minutes, she declared, "Okay, boys, you've gotten your pictures. Run along, now. A girl's got to eat!"

The photographers obliged, shoving their way back out of the pub.

Immediately, Cozy went from smiling and camera ready to strictly surly. Yanking off her sunglasses, she strode across the pub, running her beautifully manicured fingers through her glossy, black hair. She had only to nod, barely, at one of the pub waiters to make him rush to her side, a water pitcher in one hand, a green bottle in another, and a fawning smile upon his face.

"Mrs. Beckon!" the waiter trilled as he led Cozy to the best table in the house, right next to the roaring fireplace. "So nice to have you back. We've saved our finest steak for you. And, of course, here is your favorite champagne!"

"Whatever," Cozy sighed as the waiter poured her some bubbly. Then the man rushed off to the kitchen to fetch her food.

"Wow," Carmen sighed, gazing across the dining room at the imperious actress. "Imagine what it must be like to be Cozy Beckon. I bet she has a yacht and can sail wherever she wants, whenever she wants. And she probably has a home on every continent. And of course, there's the Dirk factor. He's sooooo cute—"

Suddenly, Carmen cut herself off. She'd totally forgotten she was talking to her little brother! Apprehensively, she glanced at Juni.

Maybe he wasn't paying attention, she thought hopefully. If he did, I'm in big trouble.

She was in big trouble. Juni had heard Carmen, all right. And now, he was grinning widely, working himself up into full mockery mode.

"Oooooh!" he began to hoot. "You have a *crush* on Dirk Beckon!"

Carmen closed her mouth firmly and felt her face go red. Juni's tease-fests could go on for hours! She had to cut him off at the pass.

Cozy Beckon pulled a cell phone out of her purse and began dialing, with an exaggerated display of irritability. Carmen saw an opportunity.

"Quiet!" she ordered her brother.

"Oh, you'd like that, wouldn't you," Juni said.

"Fine," Carmen hissed. "If you want to just throw away a perfect opportunity for some *spying*, be my guest."

Juni's mouth snapped shut. "*What* opportunity for spying?" he asked his sister suspiciously.

"Right there," Carmen whispered, nodding toward Cozy Beckon's fireside table.

"Hello?" Juni scoffed. "A celebrity talking on a cell phone isn't exactly earth-shattering news."

"All I'm saying," Carmen said, "is that Cozy is looking mighty agitated. And she *is* married to a Brogue United player. Maybe she knows something about our saboteur."

Juni squinted at Carmen, who was trying her best to look nonchalant.

Then he looked at Cozy, who looked simply like your average celebrity.

Juni smelled a fake-out! But he also knew the Spy Kids' mission was in trouble. If he were going to save the world—well, the world of soccer, anyway—he had to spy at every chance he got.

"Okay, you win," he grumbled to his sister. "Let's eavesdrop."

Slyly, the Spy Kids dug into their vest pockets. Each pulled out a tiny, yellow cone.

"Ah, the Uncle Machete Mini-Ear Horn," Juni whispered, gazing at the tiny device fondly. "Just stick it in your ear, point it at any person within a hundred yards, and you can hear their conversations perfectly!"

"Yup," Carmen said, popping her cone into her ear. "And it's so much more comfortable than Uncle Machete's Ear Antler."

"Not to mention, less funny-looking," Juni agreed, inserting his own ear horn.

Both kids angled their ears toward Cozy Beckon. They quickly homed in on her voice. It was so loud and clear the spies might as well have been sitting in the star's lap!

"Oh, you don't know what it's like, Kiddie," Cozy was complaining. "*Such* a bore!"

"She must be talking to Kiddie Clove," Carmen whispered to Juni. "That's Cozy's baby sister—the famous rock star."

Juni nodded and listened harder.

"Being married to a football star isn't nearly as fun as I thought it would be," Cozy went on. "It's so dull watching all those practices and scrimmages. And did you know Beckie has to go to each and every single game? What a drag!"

Cozy paused as Kiddie Clove asked her a question.

"No, I don't think I can meet you for lunch in Paris tomorrow," Cozy answered morosely. "I'm stuck in Scotland with Beckie, for who knows how long. He's got that silly old competition to attend to, you know. Between you and me, I'd *much* rather be in Hollywood, doing lunch and going to movie premieres. I mean, what's the point of being rich and famous if you have no time for any fun?"

Carmen and Juni looked at each other and raised their eyebrows.

I guess the celebrity life isn't *quite* what it's cracked up to be, Carmen thought. Either that, or Cozy Beckon is a spoiled brat!

"I swear, Kiddie," Cozy went on, breaking in to Carmen's thoughts, "I'd do *anything* to drag my husband away from this tournament. If the soccer competition could just disappear, I'd be the happiest star on earth."

As Cozy took a loud slurp of champagne, the Spy Kids gazed at each other with wide, stunned eyes.

"Did you hear that?" Juni breathed. "Cozy would do *anything* to get Dirk out of the football biz? Like, perhaps, sabotaging the competition by rigging up a false haunting!"

"And to think, I just wanted to spy on her to get you to stop teasing me," Carmen whispered back.

"I knew it!" Juni declared, triumphantly.

"Whatever," Carmen said, waving away Juni's accusing glare. "All that matters now is that my ruse has become real!"

"Yeah!" Juni replied. "We've got a suspect, and her name is Cozy Beckon!"

CHAPTER 6

Carmen and Juni sat at their table in Mackintosh's Pub digesting this new development. For a moment, they were too stunned to move or spy or even finish their desserts!

"I just can't believe it," Carmen breathed, hunching over to whisper in her brother's ear. "Cozy Beckon—a slimy saboteur. And here I thought she was kind of cool!"

"She *will* be when we expose her dastardly crime," Juni whispered back. "She'll be cooling her heels in jail!"

"Easy there, superhero," Carmen said. "May I remind you we're OSS agents? We're all about truth, justice, and fairness and stuff. We can't just swoop in and snag our suspect. We've got to have evidence against her first."

"Yeah, I guess you're right," Juni grumbled. "Okay, so we'll start by just asking her some questions."

"Now, you're talking," Carmen said. "Of course, getting to her is going to be megahard."

"Why," Juni shrugged. "She's right across the room. We just walk over there, flash our badges, and sit down."

"Juni, Juni, Juni," Carmen sighed. "You are so naïve. If we go over there, she'll totally dash. You see, when stars go to dark little dives like this one, it's because they want some privacy. They don't want to be seen, heard, or approached. They just want to silently blend into the backgr—"

"*Aaaaaaiiiigggh!*"

Carmen's eyes bulged.

"Cozy!" she gasped.

"Blend into the background, eh?" Juni said drily.

"Har-har!" Carmen responded as both spies jumped out of their chairs to go and see what had happened.

Cozy was standing next to her own chair, completely doused in red paint! Her sparkling-white pantsuit was damaged beyond repair.

Cozy pointed a trembling finger at a young man standing in front of her. The man wore a tweed jacket, a scratchy-looking vest, and itchy-looking knickers, all in different patterns of Scottish plaid. His hair was bright red and frizzy. On his face was an oily sneer. And in his hand was a large, dripping can of red paint.

"Why would you—?" Cozy stammered breathlessly. "What did I—?"

The angry young man didn't offer any explanations. He just continued to stare at Cozy Beckon defiantly.

Suddenly, recognition dawned on Cozy's face.

"Oh, I get it," she said. "You're one of those anti-fur activists who go around splashing red paint on ladies. Or throwing cream pies in the faces of mink farmers. But you've got it all wrong, buddy! I'm not wearing any fur!"

At last, the plaid-clothed plunderer spoke. And when he did, it was in a guttural, Scottish burr, complete with rolling Rs.

"Eh, please!" he sneered. "I'm not protesting furrrr."

"Then what does this mean?" Cozy demanded, snippily flicking a gob of red paint off her front.

"I will say only this," the man declared. "July 29, 2000."

"*O*-kay," Cozy said in confusion. "And what is that? Maybe that was a day you spotted me on the street. And perhaps you tried to get my autograph, but were shut out by my bodyguards.

And this is your gesture of rage and bitterness and longing."

"Wow," Juni muttered to Carmen. "I take it back. Being famous isn't cool. In fact, it makes for a really unattractively swelled head!"

The man seemed to agree.

"Don't flatterrrr yourself, Beckon," he spat. "I've said me piece. If yer smart enough to figure out what it means, *then* we'll talk. Here's where you can reach me."

The man dug into one of his garish plaid pockets and pulled out a creased and dingy business card. He flicked it at Cozy, who let the card flutter to the pub floor.

The man turned on his scuffed heel and stomped out of the restaurant.

The moment he left, the pub erupted in gasps and gossipy whispers. Cozy's obsequious waiter rushed to the star's side, carrying a bottle of sparkling water and a napkin.

"My poor Mrs. Beckon," he cried. "Let me help you. Club soda is the perfect stain remover."

The nervous waiter opened his bottle. But his hands were shaking so much the stuff fizzed all over! So now, she was paint-daubed, soda-doused, *and* hopping mad!

"This would never happen in Hollywood!" Cozy cried. She flounced out of the pub, hitting everyone in her path with drips of paint and drops of soda.

Instinctively, the Spy Kids began to follow her.

But they weren't the only ones. The horde of paparazzi had returned! As Cozy burst from the pub, the photographers swarmed around her like gnats, snapping pictures and calling out shrilly, "Mrs. Beckon! Care to comment on this public humiliation?" and "Cozy! Over here! Smile for the camera! Here, let me help with a little joke—what's rich and famous and red all over?"

"Very funny!" Cozy snarled in response. "Let me through, snottarazzi! I just want to go home!"

With that, Cozy plunged through the throng, knocking cameras and microphones out of her way as she went. An instant later—she was gone.

"Our suspect!" Juni whispered to Carmen in alarm.

"Looks like Paint Boy's escaping too," Carmen noted, pointing toward the pub's back exit. Juni turned just in time to see a flash of plaid behind the closing door.

He stepped around the paint puddles to pick up the man's business card, which Cozy had left behind.

"Malcolm MacSnaught?" Juni read with a giggle. "No wonder he's so bitter."

"You're *so* immature," Carmen sniffed, swiping the card out of Juni's hand. She glanced at it herself. Under the man's name was an address, phone number, and the title *Math and Science Genius*.

"Genius?" Carmen hooted, with a giggle of her own. "If that dude's a genius, then I'm Mary, Queen of Scots. Hee-hee!"

"Who's immature now?" Juni taunted, grabbing the card back from Carmen. He frowned. "Do you think we should include this dude in our investigation? Maybe he's a huge soccer fan and he's figured out that Cozy's a saboteur."

"How many math and science 'geniuses' do you know who like to watch sports?" Carmen asked, waving her hand dismissively. "Nah, I think this guy's just your average celebrity stalker. What we need to focus on is Cozy."

"Who's left the building," Juni reminded her as he tucked MacSnaught's business card into one of his cargo-pant pockets. "What do we do now?"

"You heard the lady," Carmen said to Juni with a sly smile. "She said she was going home."

"And so, we'll pay her a surprise visit!" Juni responded, just as sneakily.

The Spy Kids smiled at one another and set off to prepare for their little house call.

CHAPTER 7

That night, the moon cast a murky, yellow glow over the Scottish Highlands. The sky was inky and starless. On the rolling hills, craggy boulders seemed to brood and leer. A whistling wind rippled the water in the lochs—or perhaps it was the stirring of creatures beneath the surface.

All was quiet.

Eerily quiet.

Well, except for—

Khhhhrrrrggggh! EEEEEEEEEEP. EeeepEeeepEeeep!

And—

"Aaaigh! Juni! Turn that thing off!"

Carmen and Juni were crouched next to a stone wall. A moment earlier, Carmen had been shining a tiny flashlight at a recent issue of *Folks*, the gossipy magazine that followed celebrities' every move. Inside the 'zine was an article on the recently renovated Scottish castle of Dirk and Cozy Beckon. According to the story, the castle was conveniently located only minutes away from the Spy Kids' hotel. The article also helpfully noted that Dirk Beckon spent every Tuesday night with his mates at a local pub.

Luckily, it was Tuesday night! So the Spy Kids would have only Cozy to deal with as they snooped for clues.

With that information noted and the Beckon castle's coordinates keyed into her Spy Watch satellite mapping system, Carmen had been raring to get started on the mission. That was, until her concentration (and possibly an eardrum!) had been blown by the unearthly noises emanating from Juni's odd gear!

Until the contraption's earsplitting feedback jolted her out of her spy zone, Carmen hadn't really noticed it. But now, she gaped at the thing. It was a shiny, metal cap fitted firmly over Juni's messy curls. From it sprouted a tangle of metal tentacles. At the end of one of those floppy, wiry arms was a camera outfitted with night vision. Another of the device's arms had a thermometer at the tip. A third had a barometric-pressure gauge. And the fourth held a little screen filled with icons, ranging from a tiny, cartoon ghost to a weird witch to a slimy dinosaur. Beneath each icon, red, yellow, and green lights pulsed rhythmically.

"Juni?" Carmen gasped. "What is that thing on your head?"

"A ghost detector, of course," Juni said. "There's no way I am going out into this creepy night without some protection. And this baby covers all the beastly bases. The temperature and pressure gauges will detect any cold spots. And as everyone knows, encountering a cold spot on the road means you've just walked through a wandering spirit."

"*Or* a totally explainable weather pattern," Carmen scoffed. "What's the computer for?"

"It's a highly sensitive Spook-o-Meter, of course," Juni said. "If we come within a hundred yards of any of these ghoulies, the light will turn yellow. Get any closer, and it goes green. That's when I activate my ghost atomizer. . . ."

Juni held up a small weapon with a laser beam peeking out of its muzzle.

". . . *And* take a picture for OSS analysis. Not to mention *Folks* magazine," Juni said. "They pay big money for this kind of thing, you know."

Carmen gave her brother a baleful glare.

"I thought your little octopus here was for protection, not profit," she said. "How silly of me!"

"It is!" Juni replied defensively. "Mostly."

"Regardless," Carmen said, "your piggy bank is going to go hungry tonight. We've already established that our ghost isn't real. It's Cozy Beckon."

"She's the *stadium*'s ghost," Juni said. Then he gazed out across the dark, grassy hills and tightened his ghost detector's chin strap. "But we don't know about the rest of this morbid moor. I'm not taking any chances."

"Have it your way," Carmen said, pulling herself to her feet and setting off toward the castle. "Just make sure you can keep up with the mission. I have a feeling that that goofy hat is scrambling your brain!"

"Hardy-har," Juni said drily. He began following Carmen, his tentacles bouncing and rattling with every step. As Carmen stomped along, she rolled her eyes. Could her brother be any more obvious?

But as the kids trekked further into the night, Carmen couldn't help but feel a little creeped out. The gentle breeze had become a cold wind whooshing through the grass. The amber moonlight was casting long, scary shadows across the spies' path. Suddenly, Carmen shivered.

I've passed through a cold spot! she thought in panic. It's a ghost!

Squealing would have been totally unspylike.

Carmen bit her tongue and glanced shyly over her shoulder at Juni, who was close on her heels. He was so intent on his goofy ghost detector that he didn't seem to notice the wind, the shadows, or the chill in the air. Carmen felt a jealous pang in her stomach at his obliviousness. Or perhaps that was fear, gnawing at her gut!

Finally, she could remain silent no longer.

"So, uh, how's the ghost detector doing?" she asked with faux casualness. "Any . . . green lights?"

"Ha!" Juni cried in delight, pointing at his sister through his bouncing tentacles. "I *knew* you believed in ghosts!"

"Shut! Up!" Carmen hissed in response.

"Uh-oh," Juni cried, pointing off into the dark moor. "I think I see the Loch Ness monster. Boo!"

"I mean it!" Carmen whispered threateningly.

"Oh, I see. You can tease me about my ghost detector," Juni challenged his sister, "but you can't take it, eh?"

"That's not it at all!" Carmen whispered. She stopped in her tracks, grabbed Juni, and pointed off to the side. "I just mean—we've arrived at the Beckons' castle. If you don't keep it down, we'll be caught!"

"Oh," Juni whispered, cringing. In his whole

ghost quest, he'd almost forgotten why he and Carmen were on this nighttime journey! Now, he clamped his lips together as he gazed up at the celebrities' home. Of all the stony and imposing castles the kids had seen since arriving in the Highlands, this one was the stoniest and most imposing. It looked like something straight out of a bedtime story about King Arthur, except for . . .

"Hey, is that a satellite dish up on that turret?" Carmen asked, pointing at the castle's highest peak.

"Yeah," Juni said incredulously. "Right next to what looks like a big hot tub."

"Looks like our suspect has outfitted her house with all the most modern comforts," Carmen said, rolling her eyes in disgust.

"Maybe even *high-tech* ones," Juni added. "Just like the ones Cozy might have needed to rig up the stadium."

"Well, we'll know soon enough," Carmen declared, setting her jaw. "Ready to spy?"

"Ready!" Juni said, turning toward the castle. His tentacles jangled determinedly.

"Okay, I'm gonna ask you this one more time," Carmen said, pulling on one of the Spook-o-Meter arms irritably. "Are you *ready* to spy?"

"You mean . . . ?" Juni gasped, clutching at his ghost-detector helmet in horror.

"Off with it!" Carmen insisted. "That noisy thing will give us away in about five seconds."

Grumbling, Juni unstrapped the helmet and stashed it beneath a prickly shrub near the castle's heavy oak door.

Carmen pulled a heavy, lead skeleton key—complete with ominous skull and crossbones—from her spy vest.

"I got it from our innkeeper this afternoon," she explained when she saw her brother's quizzical glance. "Told him I'd locked myself out of my room. He happened to mention that this key could open half the doors in Clackmannanshire."

"Where?" Juni asked.

"That's the county we're staying in, Mr. Know-thine-enemy," Carmen scoffed.

"Let's see if the key works!" Juni piped, eager to change the subject.

Carmen slipped the heavy key into the keyhole.

It turned.

It clicked!

And then the door swung open with a creepy creak.

The Spy Kids stepped tentatively through the

doorway into a cavernous foyer bisected by a wide staircase. As the kids entered, the candles lining the walls flared up with a hiss.

"Yikes!" Juni squeaked in spite of himself.

Carmen was about to do the same when she noticed tiny red lights at the base of each wall-mounted candleholder. They were motion detectors.

"These candles are electric," she whispered to Juni. "They flared up because they sensed our presence. So calm down. There's nothing to fear here! *Aaaaagh!*"

Carmen couldn't even finish her speech before she herself jumped in terror, clutching at Juni's arm.

"What?" Juni cried.

"L—l—ook!" Carmen stuttered, pointing at the staircase with a trembling finger. There was a mummified bride, complete with moth-eaten veil, dusty, long hair, and a grisly grin!

"It's . . . it's . . ."

"It's a souvenir from a movie," Juni said with a loud guffaw.

"What?" Carmen gasped. "But it's so realistic. So grisly. So dead!"

Juni laughed again and bounded up the staircase to touch the bride's leathery arm.

"Just as I thought," he declared. "It's a latex

dummy. Don't you remember movie marathon night number four? *The Havisham Horror: Revenge of the Bride,* that extra-cheesy horror flick starring none other than . . ."

"Cozy Beckon!" Carmen said, stamping her foot. "Oh, man, I can't believe I was fooled by a movie prop!"

For once, Juni refrained from mocking his scared sib.

"Listen, it *is* really realistic," he said. "It could have fooled anyone. Even . . . the members of the American All-Stars!"

"You're right," Carmen said, bounding up the stairs to join her brother. "This would make a perfect, phony spook for the stadium!"

Juni glanced at the top of the staircase. Suddenly, he pointed at a crusty-looking oil painting mounted on the stone wall. A woman in a long, black dress and tight headband gazed sternly out of the portrait. Her lips were pursed in a little *O* of distaste.

"That painting would do nicely, too!" he declared. He ran up and stood beneath the painting of the sour old lady. Then he turned and stuck his tongue out at it.

The woman's squinty eyes rolled downward to

glare at the Spy Boy. A sticky wad of paper shot out of her mouth, hitting Juni right on the forehead.

"Hee-hee!" Juni giggled, flicking the gob away cheerfully. Clearly this prop was far from petrifying.

"Oooh, I remember that painting now, too," Carmen cried, joining Juni beneath the giant canvas. "That was a prop in Cozy's very first movie, *Spitball Spitters from Space*."

"That was an excellent picture," Juni said, nodding seriously.

"And this is excellent evidence," Carmen added. "That Cozy Beckon is our culprit. Now, we just need to track down the lady herself!"

"Or, maybe," Juni replied, his face suddenly growing white as he pointed at something over his sister's shoulder, "she's found us!"

Carmen followed Juni's gaze. In a musty corner of the hallway was another thoroughly modern amenity—a security camera, rotating on a post, with an ominous whirring sound. The camera was turning from Carmen to Juni and back to Carmen again. It was recording their every move!

"Cozy's onto us," Carmen gasped. "She's going to make a break for it now!"

"Not if we get to her first!" Juni cried. "After her!"

CHAPTER 8

The Spy Kids sprinted up the rest of the stairs. When they got to the top landing, they looked to the right and saw a shadowy corridor lined with more dour oil paintings, as well as a dozen closed doors.

When they looked to the left, they saw an old-fashioned plant conservatory—a small jungle of tropical plants under a pretty, glass dome.

Juni pointed to the conservatory. "She could be hiding under a nest of elephant ears or perched in a palm tree. She could even be swimming in a pond with a snorkel! She could be *anywhere.*"

Then he pointed down the shadowy hallway.

"And the old corridor full of doors," he continued. "That's a trick straight out of a million horror movies. You search room after room for the villain. But before you can find him, some creature jumps out of a closet and grabs you!"

Juni shivered and scowled at once. Then he announced, "Every movie, from *The Dallas Weed Whacker Incident* to *The Postman Has a Package for You,* proves it—we're doomed to fail. It is a clear-cut case of Haunted House Syndrome."

"Don't forget, Juni. We've got something all those horror movie victims don't!" Carmen declared.

"Cooler wardrobes?" Juni said, glancing down at his cargo pants and combat boots.

"Close!" Carmen said. "We've got spy skills! And they're going to lead us straight to Cozy Beckon, without any problems."

"Oh, you really think so?" Juni said skeptically. "This I gotta see."

"Watch and learn, Spy Boy," Carmen said. She reached into her vest pocket and pulled out—a fist-sized stuffed animal! It was a cartoonishly cute little bloodhound, complete with droopy ears and wrinkly snout.

"Uh, is that what I think it is?" Juni asked.

"Do you think it's a useless toy that I'm playing with at the most inappropriate moment ever?" Carmen asked.

"Well, yeah!" Juni said.

"Well, no," Carmen retorted. "It's not what you

think it is. This is *La Nariz,* another Uncle Machete original."

"The nose?" Juni translated. "What's it do?"

"Let's just say this little puppy is going to help us sniff out our saboteur," Carmen said. "That is, if we give it the right information."

"Which is?" Juni asked impatiently.

"The name of Cozy Beckon's perfume," Carmen said matter-of-factly. She began to ponder. "Now, Cozy is a celebrity, so we know her perfume's gonna be expensive. But Cozy would want something a little obscure, because she fancies herself a trend-setter. *And* it should also be a classic, because Cozy's kinda traditional."

"Y'know, Carmen," Juni said rolling his eyes. "I think you've been spending a little too much time reading *Folks* magazine. You're scarily celebrity-savvy."

Carmen managed to ignore Juni's comment. She'd just come up with a good guess as to Cozy Beckon's perfume!

"I've got it!" she said. "MallaMar. It's pricey, classy, and stylish, all at once."

Carmen typed the name of the perfume into a tiny keyboard in the bloodhound's belly. The moment she hit ENTER, the stuffed animal's head reared up. Its fuzzy, black nose sucked in a great gust of air. Finally, *La Nariz* scrambled out of Carmen's hands and began skittering down the corridor.

"You've *got* to be kidding me!" Juni said in disbelief.

"Just because it's supercute doesn't mean it won't work!" Carmen said. She bounded after the puppy. Shrugging, Juni followed the pair. And in a moment, spies and puppy were all standing before the third-from-last door of the corridor.

"See," Carmen whispered. "A totally random location. We couldn't have done it without our little helper, here."

With an affectionate smile, Carmen scooped up the robotic dog and put him in her pocket. Then she glanced at Juni.

"Ready?" she asked.

"Ready!" Juni replied.

Carmen grabbed the heavy, brass knob and pushed the door open. Rushing into the room, the Spy Kids gasped in wonder. They had just entered a sprawling and luxurious suite. The cold, Gothic windows were swathed in gauzy, pink curtains. The floor was covered in snow-white, shag carpeting. A minikitchen at one end of the room was all about stainless-steel appliances, marble countertops, and a huge stash of snack foods.

"Talk about cozy!" Juni said. "When's the last time you saw a medieval castle with its own minispa, video-game nook, lap pool, *and* swank entertainment center?"

"You're right," Carmen said, peering around the luxurious suite. "It's got everything—except Cozy!"

Carmen sniffed the air.

"But I smell MallaMar," she added. "She must have just been here!"

Suddenly, Juni detected a flicker of movement beyond the pool. He took off after it at a gallop, skidding around the long, narrow body of water just in time to see a flash of raven hair and a glimpse of someone ducking into a closet.

"Ha-ha!" Juni cackled to himself. "The first rule of any horror movie is: *Never* go into a closet. You're a sitting duck in there."

Motioning to Carmen, Juni began to walk toward Cozy's hiding place. As he tiptoed along, he imagined himself apprehending the woman. Then he pictured his face in the Spy-Kid-of-the-Month picture frame at OSS headquarters. But just when he started imagining his victory party, he heard a sound.

A sound that chilled him to the bone.

Ding!

Trembling, Juni looked up. Above the closet door was a little brass circle. And in that circle was a neon-green "3." A second later, the "3" became a "2."

"Nooooo!" Juni cried in despair. "That's no closet. It's an elevator!"

"Back downstairs!" Carmen shrieked.

The Spy Kids galloped back down the corridor.

"Activate your Automatic Rain Gear!" Carmen yelled as they ran.

"Excuse me?" Juni said. "Are you planning on taking a dip in the pond?"

"Just do it!" Carmen ordered. Then she pressed her own rain-gear button, hidden in a crease beneath her spy-vest collar. Instantly, panels of bright yellow vinyl popped out from every seam of her OSS uniform. The Spy Girl was now completely weatherproofed. But, more important, she was completely slippery!

"Whoo-hoooooooo!" Carmen cried as she jumped onto the staircase's polished, stone banister. With the help of her slick rain gear, she whizzed down the rail at super speed.

"Ingenious *and* fun," Juni gasped as he watched

his sister. "Now that's my kind of spying."

Juni pressed his own rain-gear button and skimmed down the stairway.

In fact, the Spy Kids slid so swiftly that when the banister ended they went flying. They landed in a heap on the foyer floor, right before a coat closet.

Ding!

Make that . . . an elevator! The door was opening. And behind it lurked Cozy Beckon. She was wearing a scarf over her dark locks, sunglasses over her flashing, brown eyes, and a drab trench coat. Clearly she was planning on going out unrecognized.

As Carmen and Juni leaped to their feet to stop the starlet, she thrust both palms toward their faces, blocking their vision.

She pushed her way past them and made a run for it.

But right before she reached the front door, Cozy whirled around to face the Spy Kids.

She whipped off her sunglasses and gave the kids a dazzling smile. "To what do I owe the pleasure of this little bout of breaking and entering?"

"We only want to ask you a couple of questions," Carmen said, taking a step forward. "On behalf of the OSS."

"Sure!" Cozy said, smiling again while striking a pretty pose.

Giving her brother a surprised glance, Carmen began to ask Cozy questions.

"Where were you on the night of October 22?" she asked.

"Hmmm, who can remember?" Cozy murmured. "You'll have to ask my publicist."

Carmen made a note of the reply on a small notebook she had pulled from her vest pocket.

"Why do you collect props from all your movies?" she continued.

"Oh, I don't know," Cozy said. "Most of them were gifts from my agent. You'll have to ask him."

"I also know, from *Folks* magazine, that you had two years of community college. Tell me, you didn't happen to study engineering or computer science there, did you?" Carmen asked.

"Oh, if you'd like a copy of my school transcript, I'm sure my personal assistant can help you out," Cozy answered cheerily. "Now, if you'll excuse me . . ."

And before the Spy Kids could react, Cozy suddenly turned on her spiky high heel and made a dash for the door.

"Carmen!" Juni cried. "She's getting away!"

Carmen gasped and looked up from the

notebook where she'd been scribbling away. As she saw the door close behind Cozy, she slapped her forehead.

"She pretended to answer all my interview questions," Carmen complained, "but really, she didn't say anything at all. She just distracted me."

"Whoa!" Juni breathed. "She's good."

"You don't get to be that famous if you're not," Carmen agreed darkly. "So, we've still got nothing."

"We've got nothing *here*," Juni said. "But what about back at the scene of the crime?"

"The stadium?" Carmen asked in a confused tone.

"Yeah," Juni said. "Now that we know what we're looking for, maybe we'll be able to find something that definitively links Cozy to the fake haunting."

"Good thinking," Carmen admitted, giving the front door another glance. She was completely humiliated by Cozy's maneuver. "But aren't you scared to go back to the stadium, Mr. Ghost Detector?"

"Hey, I'm a spy," Juni protested. "A professional! I don't let a case of the willies prevent me from carrying out my assigned mission."

Carmen raised her eyebrows. She had to admit she was impressed.

Bright and early the next day, Carmen and Juni arrived at the stadium, determined and optimistic. Until they walked onto the field. Then, their faces fell.

"We're all alone!" Juni cried, looking around wildly. His shrill voice echoed off the endless banks of empty bleachers.

"I guess the All-Stars canceled their practice today," Carmen said. "They're too spooked to even *try*. If we don't save the day soon, they'll be in no shape to compete against Brogue United when the Competition starts."

"So, what you're saying," Juni quavered, "is . . ."

"The situation is dire," Carmen declared. "Without these last, crucial days of practice, the All-Stars' humiliation is certain. And if that happens, the future of the American Soccer League is doomed!"

"No pressure or anything," Juni said drily.

"Want to check out the lower level?" Carmen asked.

"Sure!" Juni said.

Neither Spy Kid wanted to admit that they were just as petrified of the creepily empty field as the players were. They walked in silence down a flight of stairs to the arena's underbelly—a complicated network of sloping corridors, locker rooms, and conference halls.

One of those halls was their first stop. They wandered into the dimly lit room and gazed around. The room was outfitted with a lectern and a cluster of microphones for sports stars.

"Everything looks normal," Juni said.

"Shhh!" Carmen cried, clapping her hand over her brother's mouth.

"Wha—*mmmpphhhg*—" Juni protested.

"You had to say it, didn't you," Carmen complained. "Remember Regulation C-22?"

"Ugh! The Jinx Code," Juni groaned. "Never declare a victory—even a tiny one—in mid-mission. Sorry. I totally forgot!"

The Spy Kids gazed around the room again, wondering what horrible haunting was going to surface now that Juni had jinxed them.

They didn't have to wait long. Suddenly, the power strip leading to the microphones lit up with a red flash, and the microphones themselves crackled to life.

Finally, the speakers that were built into every room and corridor in the stadium began to echo with a horrible, creepy voice.

The voice was scratchy and gurgly, with a touch of sliminess around the Ss. Its message was not too pretty, either.

"I knoooooowwww you," the voice howled. "You are Carmen and Juni Cortez."

"Uh . . . that would be us," Juni squeaked. "Hi! And you are?"

"It's too late for pleasantries," the scratchy voice roared. "Get out, or prepare to be doused!"

"Doused?" Carmen demanded to the air. "That's not a very scary threat, is it?"

"Um, I'd beg to differ on that point," Carmen's trembling brother whispered.

"Hello?" she whispered back. "I'm trying to intimidate our foe here."

Carmen cleared her throat and turned back to the seemingly empty bank of microphones.

"Maybe we'd be more scared if you showed yourself," Carmen announced loudly. "Though, I highly doubt it!"

That ought to shame Cozy into coming out of hiding, Carmen thought smugly.

Unfortunately, the effect was just the opposite. Not only did Cozy stay hidden, she turned off every light in the stadium. The Spy Kids screamed. They grabbed each other. And *then*, they dashed out of the press room. Feeling their way in darkness through the main corridor, they began to race toward the light of the open field.

Along the way, they passed by the Brogue United locker room.

"Aaagh!" Carmen screamed, as a torrent of water shot out through the locker-room door, dousing her, as promised.

Ping! Pingpingpingping!

"Eeek!" Juni shrieked as dozens of tiny tiles suddenly popped out of the locker-room floor and whipped up toward him, hitting his arms and legs hard enough to leave stinging welts.

"Run!" both Spy Kids cried to each other.

And before any more haunts—fake or not—could scare the wits out of them, they fled the stadium for the second time!

CHAPTER 9

Carmen and Juni bolted from the basement of the stadium and sprinted out one of the arena's exits.

They kept on running, down the gravelly country lane. They petered out somewhere just outside of town.

"It looks like we lost Cozy," Carmen huffed after a moment. "We can take refuge here until we catch our breath."

"*Creepy* refuge," Juni noted, gazing around the barren countryside. "Just like everything else in this crazy country. Yikes!"

"Yeah," Carmen said wearily. "I can't believe we got scared out of the stadium not once, but twice!"

"*So* humiliating," Juni agreed. Then he looked at Carmen slyly.

An alarm clock beeped, and Juni grabbed a small radio from his pocket. "It's time for the *Star Report*," he said.

"Since when do you listen to the *Star Report*?" Carmen asked.

"Since I'm casing a supercelebrity," Juni said, grinning. "Don't you want to hear it?"

Carmen leaned in close to the radio. "Good moooooorning, Clackmannanshire," the deejay was shouting. "If you're just tuning in, then you're *just* in time for our celebrity news report."

The deejay yammered on about some star's new book, another's plastic surgery, and a third's wedding. Juni yawned loudly. Even Carmen was on the verge of clicking off the tedious report when suddenly, the deejay announced, "Sad to report that our own fair county has lost one of its glam celebs—at least until the end of the International Soccer Competition. Cozy Beckon jetted out of Edinburgh airport last night for two luxurious weeks in sunny Biarritz! The star explained her sudden vacation by saying, and I quote, 'The Competition has gotten way out of hand. Two uninvited fans even showed up at my castle last night! You can imagine how annoying, and even scary, that was! What's more, I don't want to distract my Dirk from his game. After all, I want Brogue United to beat those All-Stars. Go, team!'"

"What?" Juni gasped as an equally shocked Carmen clicked off the radio. "She thought we were *fans*? How embarrassing."

"That's *so* not the point, Juni," Carmen admonished. "Did you hear when she left the country? Last night."

"And we were terrorized at the stadium this morning," Juni said. "How could Cozy be in two places at one time? You don't think she really *is* a ghost, do you?"

"No!" Carmen scoffed. "And I also don't think she's our suspect!"

"I hate to admit this, but I think you're right!" Juni wailed. "Which means we're back to square one in our search."

"Ugh!" Juni cried. He flopped backward into the grass.

"Ouch!" he exclaimed, picking a card up from the grass and glaring at it. When he read the caption, he shook his head.

"Naturally," he complained, "it belongs to that annoying 'genius,' Malcolm MacSnaught. It must have popped out of my pocket."

Meanwhile, Carmen eyed her cell phone with the same amount of annoyance, until something on the phone's little screen caught her eye.

"Here's a call from two days ago. What's this number?" Carmen said.

"I think that's the creepy call I got in the stadium," Juni said with a shiver. "But don't worry. I already tried calling it *and* tracing it. I hit total dead ends. That's another ghostly prank, I guess. Our villain called from a number that belongs to no one."

"On the contrary," Carmen mused, "these are the fave digits of every physicist I know!"

"Huh?"

"Dude," Carmen said. "3.141592653? They're only the first ten digits of pi, which is the foundation for all algebraic thought! I can't believe you didn't notice that yesterday."

"Hey," Juni protested, "I may be an international superspy, but I'm still only in fifth grade. We haven't gotten to algebra yet."

"Whatever," Carmen said. "What I want to know is, why pi?"

"Whoever sent us that number must have been sending some sort of message," Juni said. He toyed absentmindedly with Malcolm MacSnaught's business card as he mused on the matter.

"The person would have been a real math nerd," he said. "Who else would go to so much trouble? Hmmm . . ."

Suddenly, Carmen snatched the business card out of Juni's hand.

"Hey!" Juni yelped. "You just gave me a paper cut."

"Well, you just gave *me* the answer to our mystery," Carmen said, holding up the business card. "Malcolm MacSnaught claims to be a math-and-science genius. He totally could be the one who sent us that numeric message."

Juni's mouth dropped open.

"You're right," he cried. "And Malcolm's also an angry young man. It's all adding up!"

"We need to figure out what he's so mad about!" Carmen declared.

She whipped a slender, tiny laptop computer out of the biggest pocket on her cargo pants. As she booted up, she thought back to their encounter with MacSnaught.

"Malcolm said that he wasn't protesting fur with his red-paint stunt," she noted.

"Instead, he gave Cozy a date," Juni recalled.

"July 29, 2000," Carmen declared. Briskly, she typed the digits into her computer. In an instant, she had pulled up an assortment of events associated with the date.

"Well, it's the birthday of Delilah Ruse," Carmen noted, "daughter of a superstar couple."

"Ugh, please," Juni groaned. "No more celebrity gossip. I can't take it!"

"I can't see how it would be relevant, anyway," Carmen admitted. She scrolled further through her findings. "Let's see. . . ."

Suddenly, Carmen gasped.

"Look at this," she said, angling the screen toward her brother. "Did you know that Scotland once had a secret space program? On July 29, 2000, they were supposed to launch a shuttle toward Mars!"

Carmen began typing furiously. Soon, her screen was filled with information about the Scottish Space Syndicate, otherwise known as SSS.

"It looks like the Scottish government had assembled an elite team of test pilots, scientists, and deep thinkers to make a Mars mission happen," Carmen said. She pointed to a photograph of about two dozen men and women in white lab coats and leather jackets. At the front of the crowd was a determined-looking man with a serious crew cut. He wore thick, horn-rimmed bifocals, and a vest elaborately embroidered with stars, planets, and comets. A caption beneath the photo read, "Charlie Yammer, CEO of SSS, and his team."

"Cool," Juni said, admiringly. "But obviously, the

Mars mission *didn't* happen, did it? I wonder why."

"I'll *tell* you exactly why," Carmen said, quickly scanning the rest of the document. "Because of the International Soccer Competition!"

"What?" Juni said in astonishment.

"Yup. In January 2000, there were two big items in the Scottish news," Carmen said. "One was this Mars mission, to be held in July. And the other was the competition. Scotland hosted the competition for the first time four years ago. Every man, woman, and child in the country was struck silly with football fever. They were ecstatic."

"Who wouldn't be?" Juni asked with a shrug. "So what was the prob?"

"Well, the Scottish public was so obsessed with the competition that they totally lost interest in the Mars mission," Carmen said sadly. "And without public support, the government cut the mission's funding. It took millions of pounds meant for the space program and gave it to a team of builders instead. And that's how our gigantic Stand-Off Stadium was designed and erected."

"Ouch. That's harsh!" Juni said. "What happened to all the geniuses of the SSS?"

Carmen clicked her mouse a few times until she found the genius roster.

"Let's see," she said. "Charlie Yammer, the head honcho, was snapped up by NASA. He moved to the United States. Looks like most of his team went with him or retired."

"Most?"

Carmen nodded. As she scrolled through the genius list, her face went pale. Then she croaked out the rest of her findings.

"One of the scientists, a true-blue, plaid Scot, refused to leave his homeland," she breathed. "He stayed behind, jobless, dreamless, and very angry."

"Let me guess," Juni said, clutching his stomach. "This angry scientist's name? It wouldn't be—"

"Malcolm MacSnaught," Carmen confirmed. "Otherwise known as our new lead suspect!"

CHAPTER 10

With their sleuthing energy renewed by their findings, Carmen and Juni jumped to their feet, gathered up their gear, and tracked down the address on Malcolm MacSnaught's card. When they arrived, they discovered a dilapidated little building on the edge of town. The windows were small and smudged, making it easy for the Spy Kids to peek in on the mad scientist.

They didn't know whether to gasp or laugh when they looked inside. The lab was well stocked with all the equipment necessary to create a fake haunting, from latex molds to steaming, foaming, and exploding chemicals to flesh-eating plants, gestating in an incubator.

And what made this nefarious lab different from all others? It had a rather . . . *vivid* color scheme.

"I'll say this for Malcolm," Juni said. "He sure is patriotic!"

"No kidding!" Carmen agreed. "I've never seen

a Bunsen burner painted in green-and-yellow plaid before."

"Or a refrigerator papered in red-and-blue plaid," Juni said. "Not to mention a dishwasher crisscrossed with green-and-red stripes—"

"—Or a microscope enameled in green-and-black ones," Carmen added. "This dude's got every tartan in Scotland represented here."

"But where's the man himself?" Juni wondered.

The answer came a moment later, when MacSnaught emerged from a back room, accompanied by a puff of supersmelly, green smoke. On his pockmarked face was a fiendish smile. And in his hand was a bucket filled with what looked like grass-green slime.

"That looks like the perfect stuff to smear on a soccer field," Juni said, "and trip up the players."

"It does look that way, doesn't it?" Carmen said, rubbing her hands together. "Look! Malcolm's getting ready to leave."

Carmen was right. MacSnaught had just put on a black-and-brown, plaid jacket and a red-and-blue, plaid scarf. He grabbed his bucket and flounced out the door.

The Spy Kids pressed themselves against the cottage wall until MacSnaught had moved a safe distance away. Then they began to tail him down the country lane that led out of the village.

"He's headed for the stadium," Juni whispered excitedly.

"All we have to do is follow him there, and we'll catch him red-handed," Carmen declared.

"Or green-handed," Juni said with a giggle.

"Shhhh!" Carmen said, glaring at her brother. "Do you want him to hear us?"

Juni glanced at MacSnaught, who was hustling along a hundred feet in front of the Spy Kids.

"Look at the guy," Juni scoffed. "He's so obsessed he's got no idea we're following him."

"Juni! Knock it off!" Carmen cried. "That's the *second* time you've violated the Jinx Code today. Do you ever learn?"

Juni cringed—just as Malcolm MacSnaught glanced over his shoulder and spotted them.

"Blast!" Carmen said in an angry whisper. "Our security's been compromised."

She grabbed Juni by the elbow and pulled him behind a nearby boulder.

"We'll wait here until he thinks he's lost us," Carmen said to Juni with a glare. "Then we'll use our rocket shoes to hightail it to the stadium. If we're lucky, we'll still be able to catch him in the act of sliming the field."

"Okay," Juni whispered with a guilty grimace.

The Spy Kids sat next to the boulder, stock-still and silent, for a good five minutes. Finally, Carmen peeked out from behind the big rock. There was no sign of MacSnaught. She glanced back at her brother and chirped like a cricket. That meant, of course: *Make like a cricket and hop outta here!*

Which was exactly what Juni did. But with his first hop out from behind the boulder, his legs flew out from underneath him!

"Whoaaaa!" the Spy Boy shrieked, before landing on his back with a thud. When he sat up, his back was covered in grass-colored slime!

"Aw, man," Juni complained. "Here we thought we were giving Malcolm the slip, and he was giving us one—literally!"

"Gross!" Carmen said as she helped her slippery brother to his feet. "It looks like our villain isn't just evil, he's also slippery!"

"Well, two can play at that game!" Juni said, slamming a fist into his palm.

"Don't I know it?" Carmen said drily. "What do ya got?"

"Hmmm," Juni said. "Hey, Malcolm's a nerd,

right? Why don't we hit him with Spy Maneuver #30-A?"

"The Sticks and Stones Assault?" Carmen said, biting her lip. "I don't know. As a fellow math geek, I'm morally opposed to it. Let's only use it as a last resort."

"Okay, then, what do *you* have?" Juni retorted sullenly.

"Let's just say," Carmen said, flicking some goo off Juni's shoulder with a sly grin, "that I think green really is your color."

Ten minutes later, the Spy Kids had reached the stadium. As they crept through one of the arena's entrances, Carmen was in fine villain-nabbing form. Her toes were tapping in their springy-soled combat boots. Her fingers were twitching near her utility belt of weapons. She looked serious. She looked ready. And most of all, she looked cool.

Her brother, on the other hand . . .

"I look like the biggest dweeb of all time!" Juni complained as he stumbled along next to Carmen.

"Well, maybe that'll teach you to ease up on all those 'math geek' comments," Carmen said. She couldn't even pretend that she wasn't grinning. Juni *did* look like the biggest dweeb of all time. He also looked like an alien from outer space! His face was painted green and plastered with odd lumps of cakey makeup. Rubbery points were glued to his ears. And the iridescent, green jumpsuit he was wearing was dusted with red powder—a simulation of Martian dirt.

"Malcolm will never believe I'm a real Martian in this cheesy outfit," Juni complained, tripping over his own feet in their clunky moon boots.

"Not if he sees you close up," Carmen agreed. "But from a distance, you'll seem like the real deal, which will make you Malcolm MacSnaught's Achilles' heel. The guy is space obsessed! He won't be able to resist coming out to take a closer look at you. And then, we'll snag him!"

Carmen stopped walking. The kids had reached the end of the stadium tunnel. Before she emerged into the open arena, Carmen ducked behind a couple of bleacher seats.

"Okay, Martian," she quipped to Juni. "Go to it."

With a sigh, Juni tapped his heels on the floor, causing two jets of fire to spew out of the back of his boots. Then he rode his rocket shoes into the center of the stadium, doing a few somersaults and loop-de-loops in the air as he went. He wanted to make sure he attracted MacSnaught's attention.

He landed on the center line of the field and pushed the voice-amplification button on his spy watch. When he spoke into his watch's minimike, his voice echoed through the stadium.

"Earthling-ling-ling," Juni roared. "Show your-self-self-self!"

Juni planted his green fists on his hips and waited. When nothing happened, the Spy Boy stamped his moon-booted foot and spoke into his watch again.

"Come out-out-out!" he ordered. "I will observe you-you-you and you can eyeball me-me-me!"

That turned out to be a perfect choice of words! At that very moment, a spherical object suddenly appeared at the mouth of another tunnel. The ball began rolling, by its own volition, across the field toward Juni.

Juni gaped. He felt panic well up within him. He wanted nothing more than to dash away.

But then Juni thought of the OSS, which was counting on him to complete his mission.

He thought of the terrified players and all the beleaguered American soccer fans.

Most important, Juni thought about his sister, calling him a fraidycat!

Then he squared his shoulders, focused on

truth, justice, and the American All-Stars—and stood his ground.

Such bravery was *really* hard to pull off once the ball came to a halt a few feet from Juni. Because this was no simple sphere. It was a giant eyeball, covered in craggy red veins, with a bright green iris and a malevolently squinting pupil!

The eye was giving Juni quite the once-over. Its gaze rolled from his rubbery ears to his green makeup to the visible zipper on his sparkly jumpsuit.

And then a voice—the voice of Malcolm MacSnaught—echoed through the stadium.

"Juni Corrrrrr-tez, I presume?" MacSnaught asked over the loudspeaker.

Juni cringed. Clearly this eyeball contained some sort of surveillance camera—one that had given MacSnaught a close-up of his totally fake Martian getup.

"Pleased to see you again," MacSnaught said. "But you look bored, standing in the middle of this empty field. So why don't we rrrrremedy that? Let's play ball!"

With that, the giant eye popped off the field— and began hurtling toward Juni's head!

CHAPTER 11

Juni watched the giant eyeball career toward him.

"Aaaaaagh!" he shrieked.

The slimy sphere was only inches away from splattering him right in the schnoz when Juni's spy instincts kicked in. He dived to the ground, dodging the ball and sending himself into a break dance–style spin on the grass.

Hey, this is cool! Juni thought as he whirled like a top. Of course, it'd be even cooler if MacSnaught thought I *meant* to do that.

As his spin wound down, Juni crossed his arms over his shoulders, glared broodingly, and struck a bad-boy pose.

Unfortunately, the only one in the stadium impressed with Juni's smooth move was, well, Juni.

MacSnaught's eyeball barely missed a beat. It simply veered around in the air and began hurtling back toward the Spy Boy.

Meanwhile, Carmen jumped out of her hiding spot and was shouting, "Juni! Stop horsing around! Malcolm's clearly onto us! Quit dancing and start fighting!"

Carmen vaulted onto the field and began running toward her brother. By the time the eyeball reached Juni again, Carmen was at his side, with her arms in a fighting pose.

"Hi-*yah*!" she cried, giving the eyeball a brutal punch. She knocked it away before it could mow Juni down. Juni chased after the flying eyeball and bashed it with a powerful karate kick.

The eyeball continued to fly, but it was clearly disabled. Its flight path grew wobbly and its pupil became dilated.

"Two more hits will definitely take this thing out," Carmen whispered to Juni.

"Ladies first," Juni said with a grin.

Smiling back, Carmen ran toward the eyeball. She leaped into the air and used her knee to kick the slimy thing over to her brother, in true soccer fashion.

Juni was ready. He jumped backward, flinging his feet skyward. He caught the eyeball neatly with his toe. Then he punted it right toward one of the soccer goals. The ball hit the net with intense force, then plopped onto the field and came to a halt.

"Goooooooaaaalllllll!" Juni cried in a perfect imitation of a sports announcer.

"Hey, when in a soccer stadium . . ." Carmen said with a laugh.

"Good work, kids!"

Carmen and Juni started. Malcolm MacSnaught was talking to them again, through the stadium's loudspeaker!

"So you beat my eyeball," the unseen scientist said to the kids. "Big deal. It had already told me what I wanted to know—that you're no Martian, Spy Boy!"

Juni looked at his clunky feet in shame. MacSnaught was right. His spy tactic had been a total bust.

"And it looks like your bag of tricks is pretty much empty," MacSnaught said, gloating, "whereas, *I* have countless more 'supernatural' scares up my sleeve.

"You won't possibly be able to find all of my booby traps and bogeymen," MacSnaught continued. "Which means your precious players are in for some more terror. Pretty soon, they'll forfeit their competition. The tournament will be ruined! And *I* will be watching it all from my supersecret hiding place, a place inside this very stadium that you will *also* never be able to find. It's too ingenious, too brilliant! Ah-ha-ha-HA!"

MacSnaught unleashed a maniacal cackle. It sent a shiver down Juni's spine. But it also made him think of horror movies—and all the things he had learned during the Spy Kids' horror-movie marathon.

And suddenly, Juni knew just what to do!

"Carmen," he whispered out of the side of his mouth.

"What?" she whispered back.

"What's the one thing every horror-movie villain has in common?"

"Is this any time for a trivia quiz?" Carmen hissed back.

"It's the desperate desire for acknowledgment," Juni whispered back. "They don't just want to *do* a bad deed. They want to tell you all about it. And as long as a villain has a captive audience . . ."

". . . Then he'll keep talking," Carmen finished, snapping her fingers. "So we make sure Malcolm keeps prattling on. And while he's distracted, we hunt him down."

"Yeah," Juni said. "We've got two things on our side. One—the giant eyeball can't see us anymore."

Carmen giggled, shooting the motionless sphere a smug look. "But what's the other one?"

"Uncle Machete's Sartoritron!" Juni declared, pulling a tiny device out of his pocket. The gadget looked like a digital thermometer. But instead of a bulb of mercury at its tip, it had a tiny, dish-shaped scanner.

"So you want to use the Sartoritron to flush him out?" Carmen asked.

"Exactly!" Juni said. "Let's get him bragging. He won't even know we're on his trail."

"Let's do it!" Carmen whispered. She held her hand out toward her brother. "Ready, Cortez?"

Juni slapped his hand on top of Carmen's.

"Ready, Cortez!" he answered with determination.

When the Spy Kids had completed their gesture of solidarity, they launched their plan. Juni turned on the Sartoritron and waved its scanner near his Martian outfit.

The Sartoritron's tiny screen flashed one word: SUPERGEEK.

Then Juni scanned Carmen's OSS uniform.

ULTRACOOL, the Sartoritron flashed.

"It's working like a charm," Juni confirmed with a smile.

"All right," Carmen whispered. "Now we just have to get Malcolm MacSnaught to riff about his rebellion for about ten minutes. That shouldn't be too hard. The guy's ego is enormous!"

Without further delay, Carmen raised her voice.

"You think you're brilliant, don't you, Malcolm MacSnaught?" she called out to the air. "Well, if you ask me, that speeding fireball was nothing but lame!"

"What?" MacSnaught retorted through the loudspeaker. "If you had any idea of the quantum physics, pyroengineering, and meteorology that went into these hauntings, you'd be singing another tune, lassie!"

"Oh, yeah?" Carmen yelled, shooting Juni a wink. "Try me!"

"All right!" MacSnaught replied, in a blustering tone. "I will! It all began in me lab, with a simple piece of flint and some fine Scottish peat. But the magic, y'see, was in the carbolic acid. . . ."

Carmen's ploy had totally worked! Malcolm launched into full blather mode. As he went on (and on and on) about his scientific feat, Carmen and Juni snuck off the pitch and descended into the stadium's underbelly. Juni waved the Sartoritron around as they walked.

The tiny gizmo beeped and blipped promisingly, but, from the press conference room to the showers, it came up dry.

"Let's dig deeper," Carmen suggested.

Nodding, Juni followed her down a ramp that led into an area known as "the dungeon." That was the place for soccer ball storage, heavy-duty laundry machines, and the hulking, smelly sausage carts. It was a grim and yucky place—perfect for a mad scientist.

Proving that point, the Sartoritron started beeping only seconds after the Spy Kids had descended into the dungeon. Juni looked at the gadget's screen.

NERD-O-RAMA, it flashed.

"We've got him!" Juni whispered to his sister.

Carmen looked around. The Spy Kids were standing in front of a door labeled *Brogue United Canteen*.

"Ewww!" Carmen whispered, thinking of mutton and other meats that she didn't eat. "I should have known Malcolm would choose such a disgusting hideout."

Malcolm's voice was echoing distantly over the field. "He has no idea we're here!"

"Okay," Carmen whispered to Juni. "Steady as she goes."

He nodded. He was ready.

Silently, Carmen opened the door. The Spy Kids entered a windowless, cement-floored room. It contained a maze of meat grinders, metal tables, a tall rack of recreational soccer balls, and—behind a screen, in a dark, shadowy corner—Malcolm MacSnaught! He was huddled over a microphone. And he was so intent on his boasting that he didn't sense the Spy Kids' presence until it was too late! Carmen and Juni pounced on him, cuffing him before they even had a chance—or reason—to yell, "Freeze!"

They stood before the trapped villain with their arms crossed.

"By orders of the OSS," Carmen announced, "you're under arrest, Malcolm MacSnaught!"

"Ye can't do this!" MacSnaught raved, struggling against his wrist and ankle cuffs. "Arrest a math-and-science genius such as meself, and you'll be sorry, ye snot-nosed kids."

"Oh, yeah?" Juni said.

MacSnaught didn't have a chance to answer. One of his fake haunters did the talking for him! Suddenly, every soccer ball on the rack began shooting toward the Spy Boy!

But after the whole eyeball incident, Juni was

ready. He took the ball onslaught with utter cool. One by one, he kneed, kicked, and headed every single ball away from him.

"Go, team!" Carmen cried.

Juni shot his sister a grateful grin, then glared at MacSnaught.

"Well, well," he taunted. "I guess you didn't count on my being a soccer whiz as well as a spy, did you?"

Juni waited for MacSnaught to make a snotty retort. But instead, the villain remained silent. His thin lips trembled, and his bloodshot, green eyes watered. He was so scared he couldn't utter a peep!

"What's with the big scaredy-cat act?" Juni demanded. "After all, *you* devised that lame, soccer-ball barrage!"

"That's just it," MacSnaught rasped, finally finding his voice. "I *didn't* devise that trick. That was real!"

CHAPTER 12

Did the Spy Kids scream in terror when MacSnaught made his chilling announcement? Did they flee the stadium, as they'd done before?

No way! They'd learned their lesson. Malcolm MacSnaught was a prankster and a liar. Carmen and Juni didn't care how convincingly terrified the look on his face was at that moment. He was clearly trying to put one over on them.

"You're not going to get out of this bind that easily," Carmen spat at MacSnaught. "You've just spent the past fifteen minutes bragging to us about your fake hauntings. It's on the record. You can't backpedal now!"

"The only pedaling you're gonna be doing is on a stationary bike—in jail!" Juni said as he whipped out his cell phone and began dialing.

Juni turned his back on MacSnaught to speak into the phone. "Yes, this is Agent Juni Cortez, calling OSS Headquarters regarding Mission #10E.

We have our suspect in custody. I repeat, we have our suspect in custody. Please send a helicopter to Checkpoint 25-Z. Over and out."

Juni clicked off his call, then glared over at MacSnaught.

"As in, *out* with you, MacSnaught!" he added.

"And *in* with the All-Stars," Carmen said, giving her brother a high five. "Hey, isn't it almost time for the Americans' practice?"

"It would be," Juni said, his grin fading a bit, "if our team wasn't too spooked to even approach the field."

"Well, we'll just have to tell them that we've caught our 'ghost,' won't we?" Carmen said. She grabbed the cell phone from Juni and began dialing her own triumphant phone call.

Within half an hour, Malcolm MacSnaught had been airlifted out of the stadium. And the American All-Stars had been ushered in!

But they were *not* exactly in fighting form.

The soccer stars shuffled onto the field, their faces wan and pale. Their knees were knocking, and their hands were trembling.

"Whoa," Juni whispered to Carmen. "They're in bad shape. Do you think we can convince them that their frights were phony?"

"Seeing is believing," Carmen said. She stared at the team, then chose the most frightened-looking player on the squad—a wiry forward who was sitting hunched up on the bench, his eyes darting around and his teeth chattering.

"Hey, there," she called to him gently. She pulled a soccer ball out of a bin next to the bench and tossed it to him.

Freaked though he was, the forward was powerless to resist the lure of the ball. He found himself jumping off the bench to catch the football with his knee. He bounced the ball from his knee to his ankle to his forehead.

When nothing horrible happened to him, the player grinned. And he kept on playing! Finally, he called out to one of his teammates, "Hey, maybe the ghost is gone. Field this pass, dude."

The forward kicked the ball toward a midfielder who'd been standing apprehensively on the ground. The player backed up, ready to receive the ball.

And that was when it happened.

The ball sprouted wings—wiry, black, bat's wings! Squeaking creepily, the football began to fly away.

"Aaaaaaagh!" shrieked each and every All-Star. They began running toward the stadium exit.

"Hold it!" Carmen shouted to the team. "This

haunting is a hoax. If you'll stop fleeing for just a second, I'll prove it to you!"

One of the All-Star coaches, desperate to save his team's fate, blocked his players and growled, "Listen to the Spy Girl, or you'll be benched permanently!"

Whimpering, the players obeyed and turned back to Carmen. Working quickly, Carmen pulled her Laser Net Deployer out of her spy vest. She aimed the small black rod carefully and hit a red button on the gizmo's base.

A neon-green web of lasers sprang from the deployer's tip! It flew through the air with the grace of a bird of prey. Then the net snagged the soccer ball in midair. When net and ball fell to the ground, the lasers evaporated in a puff of green dust. Juni pounced on the ball and scooped it up before it could fly away again.

Juni marched the ball over to the quivering players. He found a seam in the sphere and pried it open to reveal a tangle of wires, circuit boards, and computer chips! With the flick of a finger, Juni disconnected the crucial wire.

The ball's flapping wings ceased with a pathetic *kerchunk*. Juni dropped the dead device on the ground.

"You see," he announced to the All-Stars. "This

haunt was man-made. In fact, it was made by this man!"

Juni whipped Malcolm MacSnaught's mug shot out of his vest pocket and waved it at the All-Stars.

"He's an antisoccer, mad scientist," Juni explained to the players. "But, he's now in OSS custody. Of course, that doesn't mean our job is over."

Juni nodded at Carmen, who took over the pep talk.

"My spy partner and I are going to scour every inch of this stadium," Carmen said, "to ferret out MacSnaught's scares. And while we do that, *you guys* better start practicing. In only twenty-four hours, you've got to beat Brogue United!"

"Yay!" the All-Stars roared en masse. They hoisted the Spy Kids up on to their shoulders and ran them joyfully around the field.

And what happened when they encountered another burst of flame halfway through their victory lap? The All-Stars merely laughed and stamped the darting flame out! Then they plopped the spies onto the bench and launched themselves into an intense practice. They passed the ball with panache and kicked it with confidence. They were back on the ball!

Meanwhile, Carmen and Juni unpocketed every seeking, scanning, and searching gadget in their arsenal.

"We've got the whole day to sweep this stadium clean of frights," Juni said joyfully.

"By dinnertime," Carmen cried, "the day will be saved!"

The next day, the Spy Kids set out triumphantly for the International Soccer Competition.

"This is so cool," Juni gushed as he and Carmen traipsed down the country lane. "We caught our culprit, diffused the stadium of all its scares, *and* got VIP tickets to all five games."

"I know," Carmen said. "I *love* the whole 'mission accomplished' thing! The only thing that could make this day any better would be—"

"Carmen? Juni?"

Both Spy Kids jumped. The voice calling to them was deep. And rumbly. And Spanish!

Spinning around, Carmen and Juni shouted with joy. Both of their parents were hiking down the lane toward them! They looked chic in tartan scarves and Scottish fisherman's sweaters. They were also wearing bright, proud smiles.

After swooping their kids up with congratulatory hugs and kisses, Mom explained, "Devlin thought you might like company for your post-mission prize."

"We can watch the All-Stars dominate the Competition," Dad declared, "together!"

"Whoo-hoo!" Carmen and Juni cried, jumping up and down. Sure, they were totally independent kids—most international superspies are. But after all those creepy Scottish nights and the hair-raising scares they'd had, they were happy to have their parents by their side. Especially at an event like the International Soccer Competition! The game— viewed from a VIP turret and enhanced by lots of Scottish snacks—was going to be sweet!

Minutes after the Cortez family settled into their seats, the Americans made a brilliant kickoff.

From there, it only got better. Thrilled to be playing on a poltergeist-free field, the Americans were kicking with superstrength and pristine precision. They even scored a goal in the first quarter!

"Oooh!" Juni hooted as the American fans erupted in cheers and chants. "Brogue United just allowed a goal on their home turf. What a burn!"

No sooner had Juni's boast burst from his lips than a whooshing sound filled the air.

That whooshing soon morphed into a sizzle— accompanied by a fiery flash of light!

"Oh, no!" Carmen cried, pointing up into the sky above the stadium. "Incoming!"

CHAPTER 13

What, exactly, was incoming?

A watermelon-sized comet, that's what! It had just vaulted over one side of the stadium and was plummeting down to the playing field. In fact, it was headed straight for the soccer ball, which was bouncing across the grass after a particularly brilliant punt by an All-Star forward.

"Aaaigh!" screamed the All-Stars as they dived to the ground.

"Errr . . ." growled the Scottish players as they joined the Americans on their bellies.

"Urgle!" gulped the announcer on the stadium's P.A. system.

"Eeek!" the audience gasped.

Last but not least, the Spy Kids, in their VIP turret, sputtered, "What's going on?"

Everyone held their breath as the comet hit the field, targeting the soccer ball in a sizzling, smoking explosion!

"That soccer ball is a goner!" Juni declared, gaping at the puff of black smoke on the field.

But when the smoke and ash cleared, a moment later, the soccer ball was still intact! Only inches away from it was a small, charred crater.

"The missile missed!" Juni cheered, jumping up and down.

"Yeah, but so did we!" Carmen cried. She grabbed Juni's elbow and pulled him back into his seat. "Juni, don't you get it? This is clearly another one of Malcolm MacSnaught's fake hauntings—one we overlooked. Malcolm must have preprogrammed the comet to strike during the first game—whether he was here or not!"

"You're right!" Juni cried, gazing at the crater in horror. Several of the players had gotten to their feet. Shaking in their shin guards, they were staring at the smoking hole, too. That, of course, was when another shooting star swooped into the stadium! Once again, the comet aimed for the ball but missed it by a hair. This was small comfort to the athletes, though. With the second explosion, they started to run off the field.

It didn't take long before the audience in the bleachers began moving, too.

Then they started simmering.

And shrieking!

It was chaos! After all the Spy Kids' supersleuthing, had the fake ghost won out in the end?

Not a chance.

As the smoke cleared on the soccer field, Carmen rubbed her hands together in anger.

Juni squinted so hard he could barely see.

Mom and Dad put protective arms around their stung Spy Kids' shoulders, conveying their sympathy and indignation.

Then all four Cortezes instinctively turned to form a huddle.

"Okay, kids," Dad said, "clearly, the comets are going to keep coming until the ball is destroyed. So *we've* got to nip those balls of flame in the bud! What do you say? Shall we try Spy Maneuver #18-J?"

"Ah, yes," Mom said, nodding eagerly. "The Surf 'n' Turf. We simply use Uncle Machete's Adapto-Garden Tools to till and water the grass. They'll turn this flammable field into a wet mud slick. That'll fizzle any fireball that hits this stadium."

"Good idea," Carmen said, "but wouldn't that also ruin our soccer game? No matter how fabulous the All-Stars are, they can't exactly beat Brogue United on soggy sod."

"Of course, you are right, Carmenita," Dad said,

impatiently thumping his head with his fingertips. "But what's a better alternative?"

"Hmmm," Carmen muttered, squinting hard.

As Juni, too, pondered the problem, he murmured, "You know what this reminds me of? Horror-movie-marathon number—"

"Sixteen!" Carmen interrupted. *"The Bad-News Brahmins*!"

"Yeah!" Juni cried. "It was the best flick. A ragtag team of Indian cricket players was haunted by a ghost with a dozen arms. Every time the players turned around, the spirit was hurling some new lethal weapon at them."

At Mom and Dad's perplexed stare, Juni explained.

"You see, in the movie," Juni said quickly, "the cricket players came up with all sorts of high-tech ways to battle the ghost. But in the end—"

"—It was the simple things that won the battle for them," Carmen said. "Their strength."

"And their wits!" Juni added.

"And their skills?" Mom suggested. Carmen and Juni nodded.

"And last, but not least," Dad declared, thrusting his hand into the middle of the huddle, "their teamwork!"

With a grin, Carmen, Juni, and Mom slapped their hands on top of Dad's until they had a stack of palms.

"Who are we?" Dad cried.

"The Cortezes!" his family responded.

"And what do we do?"

"We spy!" Carmen crowed.

"And kick butt!" Juni added.

"Right!" Mom said with a crinkly smile. "Now, let's go!"

The Cortezes broke apart and dashed out of their VIP turret. Side by side, they dived onto the field, landing with four perfect somersaults. Then they hopped neatly to their feet—and just in time! Another fireball had just appeared over the edge of the stadium. Once again, it was headed straight for the ball.

"Oh, no, you don't!" Juni yelled at the comet. Then he turned to his sister. "Carmen, care for a little scrimmage?"

"You got it," Carmen called back.

The Spy Kids began to dash toward the ball.

From the opposite end of the stadium, the comet, too, raced toward the ball.

"Mom, Dad!" Juni called over his shoulder as he sprinted. "Go long! We're going to make an interception."

Grinning, Mom and Dad tapped their heels on the grass, kicking their rocket shoes into gear. Then they darted over to one of the goalposts and heaved the big net into the air.

Meanwhile, as he ran, Juni rooted around in his cargo-pant pockets.

"What are you looking for?" Carmen called over to him.

"My oven mitts," Juni said.

"Oven mitts?" his sister sputtered.

"Oh, yeah, I never leave home without 'em," Juni said, as he located the mitts and pulled them out of his pocket. One was decorated with pictures of goofy tomatoes. The other was embroidered with cans of soup. "If I ever happen upon some cookie dough or hot chocolate in my travels, I wanna be prepared."

"Whatever you say, Snack Boy," Carmen called, rolling her eyes. "But here's what I want to know. Why the oven mitts *now*? After all, we've got Freeze-Ray Guns. We've got Super Sweat. We've got force fields and exploding gum and half a dozen other comet-curtailing gizmos."

"Listen, just trust me," Juni scoffed. "Slip this mitt onto your foot and follow my lead."

Juni tossed Carmen one of the oven mitts.

Without breaking his stride, he thrust his own right foot into the other one. Shrugging, Carmen did the same.

An instant later, the kids reached the soccer ball. Skidding to a halt, they looked up. Over the heads of the cowering players, the comet was coming in for a landing!

Or maybe not.

"Ooof!" Juni shouted as he kicked with his mitted foot at the comet. He stopped the ball of flame in midair. With all the flair of a future Dirk Beckon, Juni juggled the comet on the tip of his toe. While the comet continued to sputter and sizzle, his foot inside the oven mitt remained cool as a cucumber—just like the rest of the Spy Boy! Suavely, he passed the comet to Carmen.

"All right!" Carmen cried as she caught the fireball with *her* oven mitt. She punted it back across the field to her brother, then ran toward her parents, who were hovering in the end zone with the goal.

Juni caught the comet with his heel, then flipped it over the back of his head, Pelé style.

Not to be outdone, Carmen hurled herself backward and punted the fireball down the field before landing on the ground with a grunt.

Juni darted ahead and caught the ball again. Balancing it on his oven mitt, he looked down at the comet. Its orange flames had dulled and died down a bit.

"Just as I expected," Juni muttered to himself happily. "All that airtime has cooled our fireball's jets. It's starting to flame out! Which means it's time for . . ."

Suddenly, Juni adopted the resonant voice of an imaginary British sports announcer.

". . . Time for Juni Cortez, the star forward of the American All-Stars, to make his move," Juni announced with a grin. He bobbled the fireball on his toe and glanced up at the goal, hovering above him.

"And now Cortez sizes up his target," Juni "announced." "He's got mere seconds on the clock. If he makes this goal, he'll be a national hero. Will he make it, ladies and gentlemen? Or will the All-Stars—"

"Juni!" Carmen bellowed from her perch down the field. "Are you gonna save the day, or are you gonna *talk* about it?"

"Hey," Juni protested. "I was just getting there."

By now, the fireball was looking gray and ashen. It was the perfect time to—

"Shoot!" Juni cried, kicking the ball toward his parents. Mom and Dad flew into the comet's path, neatly scooping up the fizzling fireball.

"He scores!" Juni cried, running in elated circles around the end zone. "Goal! Goal! Go—oh, no!"

Fwoooom!

You guessed it. All that sports announcing had only given another comet a chance to fire itself up and soar into the stadium. It was headed straight for Carmen!

Desperately, Juni glanced at his parents.

"No problemo," Dad called down to his son. "We'll hit this one with Spy Maneuver #31-K."

"The Happy Birthday?" Juni said. "Of course! It's perfect! But can you give me a lift? I've got an oven mitt over my own rocket shoes."

"Of course, sweetie," Mom said sweetly. "You know you can always count on us when you need a ride."

Mom and Dad swooped down and grabbed Juni under both arms. As they flew, Mom reached into her pocket and pulled out four mints.

"I think we need a little fresh air," she cracked as she handed Juni and Dad a mint each.

"Make that a *lot* of fresh air," Juni said, gazing admiringly at the mint's wrapper: *Zephyr mints, by*

Machete Cortez, the label read. *Excellent for political speeches, birthday parties at retirement homes, or any occasion that requires a lot of wind.*

"Sweet," Juni said, popping the bright blue candy into his mouth. "Literally!"

The trio landed next to Carmen, and Mom promptly popped a Zephyr mint into her daughter's mouth. Then all four spies fearlessly faced the comet.

"Make a wish!" Carmen yelled as the fireball bore down upon them.

The Cortezes puckered their lips and blew.

Whoooooosh!

The force of their fortified breath was so strong that not only was the comet extinguished, but its ashes hurtled down the field and cascaded into the other soccer goal.

"*Another* brilliant score," Juni declared. He'd put on his British sports announcer voice again.

"Time for one more!" Carmen said cheerfully. She pointed into the sky. Comet number five was heading toward them.

"No problemo!" Juni cried.

Indeed! The spies hit the next comet with Uncle Machete's Super-Foamy Fire Extinguisher. The fireball that came after that was put out by Spy

Maneuver #12-J, the Tidal Wave. And *that* gave Carmen the idea to take out the *next* comet with the audience's help. Pulling one of Uncle Machete's Mini-Megaphones out of her pocket, she exhorted the crowd to make a wave. The stunned fans complied, throwing their arms up and lowering them again in perfect rhythm. All of the flapping rippling through the stands created such a breeze that comets number ten, eleven, and twelve were extinguished before they could even reach the field.

When the twelfth fireball had fizzled, the stadium finally went silent.

The Cortezes glanced at each other.

"Well," Juni said cautiously. "Do you think we finally outlasted the 'ghost'?"

"I don't know," Mom said with a shrug. "But I do know this. If it gives us any more surprises, we'll be ready!"

"Yeah," Carmen agreed. "There's no haunting we can't handle."

Smiling confidently, Carmen flipped her megaphone on again. She turned to the footballers.

"All-Stars," she said. "Broguesters. We've got the comets covered. Which means it's time for you to *play ball!*"

"Whooooooo!" the crowd roared.

The soccer players pumped their fists in triumph and took the field. They launched back into their game as the spies walked to the sidelines, arm in arm.

"You see, children," Dad cried. "You did it! You saved the International Soccer Competition *and* the morale of all the fans in the stadium. Can you hear them cheering for the All-Stars?"

Grinning, Carmen and Juni cocked their heads to listen. But when they heard the words the crowd was chanting, their jaws dropped.

"Team!" one section of the stands was shouting.

"Cortez!" called another section.

"Team!"

"Cortez!"

"Team Cortez! Team Cortez! Yayyyyyy!" the audience roared.

"Team Cortez," Juni said, grinning at his family. "That's got a nice ring to it, don't you think?"

Carmen grinned. She even threw an arm around her little brother's shoulders. Just this once, she thought, she could stand a little mushy stuff.

"It sounds," she declared, "like this team can't lose."